Currently studying anthropology and archaeology, Anfal Sheyx hopes to further her career in academics as well as writing. She loves iced coffee, shopping and travelling, and looks forward to using her writing career to justify doing all those things. Anfal Sheyx hopes to travel before moving back to her home city of London, where she plans to write many more books.

To my family: my home is wherever you are.

Anfal Sheyx

# TRAGEDY ON THE HILL

AUSTIN MACAULEY PUBLISHERS™

LONDON • CAMBRIDGE • NEW YORK • SHARJAH

A CIP catalogue record for this title is available from the British Library.

ISBN 9781035824786 (Paperback)
ISBN 9781035824793 (ePub e-book)

www.austinmacauley.com

First Published 2023
Austin Macauley Publishers Ltd®
1 Canada Square
Canary Wharf
London
E14 5AA

# Part One

# Chapter 1
# Families

It was a late day in June when he drove the young lady over. He remembered because it was an unusually perfect day on the mainland, and of course, when questioned about it days later, such details, he thinks now, were of great importance. The lady in question was dressed head to toe in blue. He likened it to the clear sky that day, or perhaps the clear water they travelled over.

He admits now, sitting over the dinner table with his wife years later, that he fancied himself somewhat smug in the way of reading people; his many years of bringing folks to and fro the mainland allowing him a special insight. It is important to note that his wife scoffed at this point in his story.

But nevertheless, the captain continued. The lady in question, he noted, he had never seen before; her clothes being more modern and fashionable, he assumed her to be from the city. What she was doing here, even he couldn't guess; but judging by the number of carry-ons he had helped to lift, she was planning on staying a while.

But if the lady in blue had reservations about being under such observation, she did not voice them but only remained looking forwards out into the ocean, towards her destination.

The chunk of rock, that in the captains' eyes could only be described as rubble, perhaps archaic if a passenger felt kind; the Newham Hill seemed to fall more silent as they steadily approached it. The stretch of land on the, well, supposed 'island' lacked the vitality and life of the mainland.

The opposed houses that stood on it, seeming to grow increasingly larger. The captain admittedly never having been a sociable person, but feeling awkward in such silence, commented on the uniqueness of having bought over two people in two months to Newham Hill. It was, he remarked, one of the only times he had ever heard the young woman speak, and her face, which he once thought plain, came alive—as did her inquisition.

"And why should that be so rare? You are a boat captain after all, or I am to believe you sneaked on this boat to operate it for the joy alone?"

It was at that moment that the slightly younger woman sitting beside her—that he almost always forgets to remark upon when recalling this story—turned her chin slightly around, and by the weight of her shoulders, he could only imagine her sigh.

The question posed, he supposed had not been answered, and he—the questioned—remembered why he did not usually like to talk to passengers, especially all-knowing city people. As the young lady's clear eyes stared at him, still in wonder, he remembered himself.

"It's just that, Miss—"

"Miss Quinn, and this next to me is Miss Abbott."

The younger woman at her side now felt the reluctant invitation to introduce herself. "Pleased to meet you."

He supposed he looked somewhat annoyed, but continued, "Miss Quinn, and Miss Abbott, not many people visit this rock. It's just the family that lives there mostly, and well, bringing two newcomers here is strange for me, you might say."

"Well, I don't know why you don't visit more often, it looks to me like the perfect little holiday spot."

The captain eyed the rock eerily as they quickly approached. As a wise older man, his wife scoffed at this too, he knew that there are days in a man's life that strike him forever; periods, if he were so unlucky, and as he reproached the boat back to the mainland, he knew that what was about to happen would strike the whole town.

It was at this point, his wife took away his whiskey.

Miss Quinn and Miss Abbott, however, upon seeing the mountain of steps they eventually were to overcome, chose instead to watch the captain as he docked away.

Miss Quinn, as always, was the first to speak. "What an interesting fellow," she remarked before hastily taking her suitcases up the stairs.

Miss Abbott, who had known Miss Quinn since childhood, knew that most people were 'interesting' to Miss Quinn, not because of their dress, or their occupation, but because of the things she often made them say, often by making them feel uncomfortable. Still, she continued.

"That's strange, don't you think? That a boat captain, who's quite possibly lived and worked in this town for decades, is so surprised to see just two people come over to this island? I mean, look at these houses! They must have been built centuries ago; they have legacies, they require upkeep and yet not a single soul comes over so often? No lawyers or builders? Or friends even?"

The very exhausted Miss Abbott only realised it was her turn to speak once her friend faced her and gave her those big eyes of wonder. She wondered how it was possible that the same pair of big baby blue eyes that got them into trouble so often as children, could so quickly get them out of it? Still, she recognised that she would certainly not be forgiven should she not offer an opinion.

"Perhaps the family likes their privacy."

"*Families*, look, Lottie! Two separate estates on one stretch of land, isn't that strange? That one should like their privacy so much as to move far from the mainland, but right next to another family. Contradictory, isn't it?"

She thought back on and remarked on the view of two separate paths and houses facing their backs to each other just as their view on the boat. As they approached the house, and finally, finally! Lottie thought away from the tortuous set of stairs, she finally noticed the house in front of them and much more ominously, the stretch of forest and wall behind it.

"Why, you're certainly right, Lottie, someone likes their privacy. Now, let's go meet our host, shall we? And let us pray that they may be more unimposing that their property."

As they entered the bright, glistening hall however Lottie decided that the host must be less imposing than their property, for the exterior of the house, while undeniably looking close to ruins, the manor was more than made up for by the brighter, more hospitable exterior. As she turned to remark that to Miss Quinn, she noticed that her friend wore a quivering brow and decided it was in her best interest not to inquire.

Instead, focusing her attention on the light colours of the hall, the fresh flowers in the vase and the perfectly hung picture frames in the ornate hallway, the frames of which matched perfectly with the wooden carpeting; Lottie realised it reminded her of immaculately decorated homes in catalogues and advertisements.

"Hello!" Before Lottie had a second longer to enjoy the anonymity and anxiety of newly invading a stranger's home, Miss Quinn announced their presence.

Nearly half a second later, their hostess revealed herself in the form of a near shrivelling voice and what Miss Abbott assumed to be a fantastic, but expensive dress, only slightly outshined by the diamond on her finger.

"Please, call me Cecilia! Oh, I do hope you found the trip alright. That captain can be a pain at times."

"It was just perfect, don't you worry. Terribly sorry about barging in, we did try knocking, but I can imagine in a house vast as this, it must be hard to hear us. Is that right, Lottie?"

Lottie, who knew that they most definitely did not knock, but who also knew of Miss Quinn's habit of entering where she pleased simply because she 'probably won't be caught', knew the course of less resistance was to agree. So, she nodded simply, and as she did, she noticed Cecilia's smile, outlined by red lipstick, as was the current fashion.

It is common knowledge that when meeting new people, after the introductions and casual conversations about the weather of course, there tends to be a silence which one can either fill with mindless chatter, or to better describe the scenario. In the hallway that day, one can simply stare in silence, begging for an intervention, any intervention; luckily, for them all, one came in the form of a sharp suit and rather poignant moustache.

Cecilia was the first to be explicitly grateful for the older gentlemen that entered. "Eddie! Oh, Eddie, there you are! These are our guests, the ones you rented the rooms out to. Remember, darling?"

The man in front of them, who Miss Abbott was sure, certainly remembered no such thing, and was definitely surprised to see strangers in his hallway, introduced himself, nevertheless.

"Eddie Newham, pleased to meet you both." He extended his hand, and shook both of theirs.

"Miss Quinn, and this is Miss Abbott." The aforementioned Miss Abbott extended her hand to reach the gentleman, being struck certainly by his height, but by his homely welcoming exterior. A smile she could relate to her grandparents, her father and old Mr Watson, their local bookshop owner.

Before she could pin his hospitable exterior down, and she later realised for the fear of another long pause, her and Miss Quinn were promptly taken to their respective rooms to settle in and unpack before being told that dinner, for their comfort, was to be at seven o'clock, and if they were hungry beforehand.

Miss Quinn decidedly expressed that they were not hungry after their long trip, and that seven o'clock was just perfect. They were left alone to their things then.

"What interesting people, Lottie."

"I don't know. I'm not so sure what's so interesting about them, they seem like a perfectly lovely couple to me."

"Well, a couple can be both lovely and interesting."

"Yes, well, except…"

Miss Quinn, who had already abandoned packing, sat on the bed, waiting for Miss Abbott to continue.

"Except that, well, some people might say that…" A quick look in the direction of the door informed Miss Quinn.

"Ah, I see, their age. Some people might find it indecent to date a younger woman, or worse, scandalous to date an older man."

Miss Abbott flinched and looked at the door, which remained ajar. Miss Quinn, however, needlessly continued her thoughts, twirling her hair, still laying on the bed.

"Her home is very curious if you've noticed. The open laid out hallway, but then the dark dingy stairs. Would you call that a renovation or a tragic clash of personalities? Assuming, of course, that the bright interior is a choice of Cecilia's. What do you think, Lottie? Lottie?"

Lottie, from whose ears the invocation went in and out, had decidedly no thoughts on the interior work of their hosts, who by all accounts seemed welcoming, if a little disorganised. A quality Lottie always frowned upon.

"Oh, I don't know, Miss. Perhaps the lady is trying to make her home here."

"Ah, I see you noticed the ring too, quite a diamond. There's this cousin of mine who always said she would never marry a man with a ring smaller than a small asteroid. If I didn't know better, I'd think she's referring to that."

"What a mindset for a woman to have. It's not all about money for some people, it's about compassion and love and empathy despite the disagreements."

"Perhaps, but goodness! Wouldn't a rock like that help the disagreements!"

"I suppose I know where you lie, Miss."

"On the engagement side? I'm undecided but couldn't tell you my mind would be swayed by some jewellery. Useless though, not as if any man nowadays has any taste. No, I would want to be taken to the store myself to pick out whatever I liked!"

"Of course, you would, Miss, you would want the whole store!" Any thoughts of organisation had been abandoned to this point, as they both sat giggling on the bed.

"There's nothing wrong with asking the world from a man, if he really wants to marry you that is."

"And if he doesn't?"

"Well then, you find a man with a slightly larger meteor then. But you won't have to worry about that, Lottie, you're gonna marry the man who'll give you the world."

Lottie's quiet smile signalled the end of the conversation. It was a topic she worried about every now and then. She loved her job, but she assumed she couldn't be a lady's maid forever. But she, more than anyone, knew how hard it was to find a man like that.

"Did she ever get married, Miss?"

"Sorry?"

"Your cousin; did she find a man who could give her the world?"

"Yes, but she had to learn to give herself the world anyway."

# Chapter 2
# The Man in Green

Dinner, as it seemed, was an event. Miss Quinn could have bet anything that she counted two people on her way in. Yet she sat on a table surrounded by more individuals than she had the energy to talk to. An ungodly 5. The 'older gentleman', as he had been dubbed by Lottie, sat at the head of the table, while his shining soon-to-be new wife, who had by some miracle had the time to slip on an entirely new dress, sat at the other end, seemingly miles away.

A strange tradition she always thought—to have husband and wife so far apart, but the hosts seemed happy enough.

It was the others, the next-door neighbours, she immediately dubbed to be more interesting. Seated next to Eddie was Miss Rebecca Beaumont—now Burton—a woman tall for her age with darker hair and light eyes, whose presence overtook the room. Her physical age made up for in her vibrant, youthful personality.

Rebecca, for she insisted both Miss Quinn and Miss Abbott call her so, sat across her husband, Hugo. Lottie, she imagined, would describe him as an appropriately older, somewhat withdrawn, gentleman, who scribbled on his napkin every few moments when he wasn't pretending to be involved in the conversation. She took him to be an inventor of some kind.

It was Rebecca, of course, whose eyes she kept getting drawn back into. It was her smile, now directed at Eddie, she decided was the source of her energy. They were currently leaning closer, exchanging stories, what she didn't know about, be it the long journey here, or her general lack of excitement when meeting people, but she hadn't said a word in a while and nobody seemed to mind.

Lottie, sitting next to Rebecca, had also seemingly picked up on the closeness and directed her attention instead to the doctor across from her. A nice older man, a friend of the family it seemed, who was engrossed in stories surrounding his practice and some of his favourite patients; to an extent that Miss Quinn became sure it must be a breach of some confidentiality agreement, but she wasn't going to stop him.

It was the last person she looked at around the table, that should've been the first. Sitting across from her, with eyes similarly scanning the table, was a girl, perhaps she should've referred to her as a woman, but a girl seemed to fit her better. Compared to the chattery table with older company talking about their life experiences, their upbringing, their best memories, she was at the peak of it all.

She seemed to Miss Quinn at the time to be like a child on the adults' table, at completely different sides of life. Jackie, as she was called, was yet to make all these memories, and was seemingly barely out of her upbringing. She could see it in her gait, sure of herself, of course, but sitting at that table observing the interactions of others, she seemed to Miss Quinn to still be unsure of who she is, as most young people are.

She followed Jackie's gaze around the table, from Rebecca to Eddie, to Hugo to the doctor; as if she was deciding her future at that moment, was she to be happy, successful, creative or by self-admittance, forgetful—alright fair enough—she had yet to figure out the doctor.

She herself had trouble following the different conversations. It was only when she heard talk of sailing that she felt fit to get involved, or as she premeditated, become involved through Miss Abbott.

"Miss Quinn is an avid sailor, Eddie, you must take her out!"

"I would be delighted, perhaps next week when you've had some time to settle in."

"Sounds perfect."

"Eddie has always been a great sailor. You wouldn't even believe how scared of the water he was when we were kids!" Rebecca chimed in, and suddenly stories of their childhoods were all that could be poured out. While on the other side of the table sat Cecilia watching it all unfold, with a full drink in her hand.

It struck her as an incredible group of people; incredible in the sense that they happened to be at the same table. Had Miss Quinn been listening, as Lottie later informed her, their involvement in each other's lives was no mystery. But for the present being, it seemed Miss Quinn lacked the attention span, much like the inventor, to focus. That was until something interesting happened, something that sparked even her attention.

The abrupt slamming of the door brought a sudden interruption of their ever-idyllic dinner. A young man with darker clothes and even darker presence brought strode in. If his misshapen tie, and tired eyes didn't give him away, the smell of smoke and alcohol coming from him certainly did. Hardly minding the company he was intruding into, the man instantly headed for what all of them must assume to be a container of whiskey.

"Daniel." The intruder only carried on his actions, hardly having the decency to pour his drink in a cup; his name only serving to accentuating the silence of the room, Miss Quinn had never realised how big that dining room was until that very moment.

"Daniel." The name now, realising came from Rebecca. This time, the young man turned around. Miss Quinn had been fortunate enough all her life never to have encountered death—her parents were alive and well, her friends healthy, even her grandparents seemed to her to be immortal. But in this moment, as 'Daniel' took in the sight of the new strangers, Miss Quinn had never realised that death could stare back at her.

"Please, have some decency and say hello to our guests."

"Thank you, Mother. But I assured you, I won't be staying long, so there's no need."

Poor Miss Abbot relaxed at the indication of the relation, as she looked about one jump away from phoning the local police. The man was gone as quickly and abruptly as he entered, but the atmosphere of the evening never quite returned. Surprisingly, it was the woman opposing her that spoke first.

"I wouldn't worry about him. I've been here a month nearly and he's never greeted me once."

"You must excuse my Daniel. He very badly misses the city. I'm making him stay here you see."

In response to the confession, it was Hugo, a man who couldn't ignore his son, who finally spoke up.

"He's a good boy, been in the city for many years though. Promised us to stay here and stay sober this summer. As you can see, it's going just fine."

"Yes, what a charming young man." Miss Quinn didn't know if the sarcasm in her voice was ignored or overlooked, but the others soon moved on.

The rest of the evening was adorned with tales of Daniel. How he was such a smart child and how his parents didn't want to suffocate him, and how as a smart young adult, he moved to the city where he could flourish. Instead of art and music though, his skills in drinking and gambling flourished. It was the first time all night that Miss Quinn finally found someone worth paying attention to.

As lovely and confusing as this evening evidently was, Miss Quinn kept seeing one glaring singularity to come back to. The woman sat across her seemed so distant from the other adults; so bright and yet wondrous, her connexion to them made another mystery altogether. How could a girl on the brink of her entire life be connected to these strangers; these idyllic figures of what would possibly become her future?

It was not it was not enough to assume a passing acquaintance, according to the ship captain tell anyone ever came here. So, what was the mystery of this young girl who had somehow stumbled her way into this glistening world; this world that could only seem to exist so in picture books and fairy tales. If it wasn't for the intrusion of the young man, Miss Quinn would be sure the entire holiday she mapped in her head would be a dream.

But again, as Miss Abbott would remind her later, if Miss Quinn had really listened instead of observing, so she would know that the mystery of young Miss Jackie was not a real mystery at all. This young woman, who sat opposing her, was no stranger to the family, and now she realised that young Miss Jackie had not stared out of animosity, but out of curiosity and intimate insight knowledge of these families.

Two curiosities, Miss Quinn decided, and later pressed.

"Jackie? Oh yes, she's known our family for quite a while, although she never came back quite until now. She lived with us here when she was just a little girl. Her mother was a maid and took care of my father for his few years."

"Your father, Rebecca?"

It was at this point that Jackie chimed into her own story. "Oh, yes. Her father. You didn't think she was self-made, did you?"

The insult seemed to be ignored as she carried on.

"Oh yes, you've caught me out, Jackie, but you already knew that, didn't you? You see, Miss Quinn, papa made his money in oil over the decades, and as soon as I was born, he packed it all up and moved us here. It was only when he got very ill towards the end that he even permitted doctors and carers to come here. Oh, but we're so grateful to have our Jackie come visit!"

"And I am so happy to be here! Although, I must say it doesn't feel quite the same without Mr Beaumont. He was so kind to me, and he died so suddenly, didn't he, Rebecca?"

"Oh yes, I suppose, but he was so ill for such a while, poor papa." Miss Quinn swore it was the first time she saw Hugo look up from his scampered napkin to comfort his wife, as well as speak up as rarely as he did.

22

"It's funny, we named Daniel after him, but Rebecca always says they couldn't be less alike."

"He's gone, but he hangs over all of you." She didn't process the words before recognising they were hers.

The pause that followed was an inclination, as always, that she had said something inappropriate.

"Maybe we should clean up. Eddie and I don't have maids here anymore. We're moving you see, so I hope you all don't mind pitching in."

Cecilia and Miss Quinn were the first to stand, their escape from the dining hall couldn't come quicker. They walked their way to the kitchen which stood at the front of the house. From the window they could almost see Daniel the junior. Standing in his discoloured suit, he looked over the edge, lighting a cigarette from the most unique little lighter Miss Quinn thought she had ever seen.

"I don't take it you ever met him. Daniel the senior?" Her words accompanying their descent into the kitchen.

"Oh, God, no. Eddie and I have known each other for half a year now, and anyway I would have been too young…God, I don't know what you must think of me, younger woman, older man with money. But I don't care about the money you see; I only love Eddie. I didn't even want to come back here, but he insisted to sell the house. Then we're going to travel the world, where it won't matter as much!"

"But it matters here?"

"To Eddie, I think it does. I've done my best but ever since we came here; he's been so ashamed."

Miss Quinn who had never had the correct temperament to deal with the emotions of people, could only take the champagne glasses, pouring over the leftovers and handing one to Cecilia.

"To a better tomorrow then," was all that could be said.

# Chapter 3
# Cradling Rocks

Tomorrow, Miss Quinn decided was not better. For a lack of clear mind and the nausea that comes with having a fun and/or boring dinner, she awoke with not much motivation to start the day. Upon being reminded by Miss Abbott that they both had an obligation to go sailing—the thought of which made her feel even worse—she resigned herself to her bed.

"Sailing? I had thought Eddie suggested next week?"

"Oh, he did, but he insisted later that we must see the whole island as soon as possible, and it's always much nicer in the morning!"

"The morning? Oh, why must things always be nicer in the morning? Why never at night or the acceptable afternoon? This is a holiday after all!" Miss Abbott ignored Miss Quinn as she rolled her eyes, tucking herself further back into bed as Miss Abbott continued her musings.

"…and you know, I think I may have misjudged Cecilia and Eddie; they seem sweet together. Though him and Rebecca seem cosy, I wouldn't like that at all although that's what happens after knowing each other so many years. Are you listening? Oh, but Rebecca is so lovely. I couldn't even accuse her of such a thing; bit of a strange husband though, but what can you expect from those inventor types.

"Though the girl seemed a little off, very tense the whole dinner, poor thing. She looked like she hadn't slept in years. Bit of a random occurrence for her to come back after all these years, isn't it? Miss Quinn? Miss Quinn."

"Lottie, I assure you, there is nothing amiss or interesting going on here. We spent the entire night with them, and they are perfectly ordinary uninteresting people; except for perhaps Jackie. She doesn't quite fit into this world now, does she?"

"No, I suppose you're right. Well, come on, then! Suppose we should get to the beach; Eddie was very pertinent about meeting us there."

"Clearly not pertinent enough to show up on time," Miss Quinn only commented, shrinking her eyes from the brightness of the sun.

"Don't be rude, he's just coming," Miss Abbott hushed.

A treacherous half hour later, both ladies stood at the shore; one beaming with excitement, the other praying for a short, short trip; the long stairs down had been hell enough. It was then that they spotted Eddie heading down the stairs after them. Unnoticeable before, he blended into the scenery of the beach with his lighter clothes, he came running down with a sweat, no doubt a scout boy as he embarrassed to have lost track of the time.

His presence was met with a thankful exclamation that they had not in fact been waiting for him long, and that all was forgiven, mostly for the humorous image of him running hurriedly down the stairs, but Miss Quinn had been told multiple times such things were indecent and awkward to comment on.

"I had already meant to have our speedboat on the water, but if you excuse the tardiness, I might actually do with some help. It does seem to be a little heavy. It's just in the shed we keep in the corner of our land."

"Must be awkward to have a boat around here, isn't it? It's only a small island," Lottie noted as Miss Quinn silently grabbed the edge of the boat.

"A small island with a lot of protection; you've no doubt noticed the wall. Impenetrable thing. Rebecca's father had it built the second they moved here. You'd need to walk down the long stairs on our end and round the beach to their side and walk up those stairs before getting in."

"Yes, we had noticed that," Miss Quinn interjected.

"How horrid! Had Rebecca's mother not stepped in?" Miss Abbott was always better at exclaims of outrage than she was.

"Mother?" In a distracted manner, Eddie unlocked the shed, prying the boat out from the under its rock of a hiding place.

"Oh, Rebecca had no mother. She died in labour I'd always heard. I suppose old Mr Daniel must've been afraid of losing his daughter too."

The combined effort of all three of them allowed for the swift—yet Miss Quinn would still utter—tiring advancement of the boat into the water, and their further hasty incline into a boat Miss Quinn was sure hadn't been touched for decades. It was only after Eddie's admittance of fear, that she chose to further the conversation as they finally set out onto the water.

Even she had to admit that an early morning sail and interesting conversation wasn't so bad.

"You've known her for a while, then?"

"Oh yes, since we were children. On a lonely island like this, we were all we had; playing out in the garden, running around each other when we weren't running away from our tutors."

"You must've known her father too then?"

"Oh yes, terrible grump. Never let anyone near Rebecca. Never liked me, that's for sure. He kept her sheltered from everything good in this world. No sympathy from me when he died either, at least Rebecca would be free, I thought."

"How did he die?"

"He'd had a stroke I believe; died a few weeks later in his sleep. I did my best to console her, but a few months later, a handsome inventor chap shows up and the next thing you know, she's married with a baby on the way."

"That must have been hard."

"Hard time for everyone, most of all the chap who's dead, I suppose. Anyway, it was all so long ago, it feels like we were different people then."

"And Jackie? You must have known her too." Miss Quinn seized her shot.

"Oh yes, but she was only a little girl then, seven or eight maybe. She took a real disliking to that house, more so when the old chap died. So as soon as her mothers work was done—the patient being dead and all—they both moved on."

But as people of their standing often do, they realised quite quickly that the topic was too cavalier for such a lovely morning and so they tread lighter, onto topics of occupation, weather and hobbies; things that unlike their morbid conversation, could be easily forgotten and not given another thought.

The sun rose higher as the water levelled out and they found a sense of calm among the sea surrounding them. However, as life usually goes, after the mastery of a great hobby, one is often compelled and boredom and then completion. Lucky for them, it was closer to lunchtime. And their conclusive opinion was that it was as good a reason as any; and with that, dawned the sad realisation that they would have to drag the boat back into the shed.

Miss Quinn felt the air breeze past her angrily as she pulled the boat out of the water. Was it this angry when they had left the dock? It had only been half an hour, hadn't it? The air bit her and chilled her skin as it rippled again.

"Wait! Did you hear that?" It was Miss Abbott, as they would later report, who heard the noise first, as she sprang up, her eyes wide.

"Hear what, Lottie?" She could feel the air change; perhaps the clouds had come in and the sun had hidden, she remembered thinking.

"I could have sworn I heard the most chilling cry!" As often as people have been tricked by their minds, the ghostly look in Miss Abbot's eyes made her inclined to believe her. Yet, she need not describe the exclamation, as a second later, it repeated itself tenfold. A cry that one only hears once, perhaps unluckily, twice in a lifetime. A cry that terrified mothers in the middle of the night; that was exclaimed by dead lover's past.

She felt it; this was death. A cry that can only signal such deep pain and loss; a cry that raises alarm and makes bystanders pray never to hear it again echoed over the island.

It was then that Eddie bent his head around the corner of the shed, his brows furrowed and his eyes haunted; while the rest of them froze, he was the first brave enough to move.

"What on earth happened? It sounds like its coming from Rebecca's side. Come on, we have to hurry!"

It was later when Miss Abbott would have to repeat the story, for police or news articles and such, that she would say her mother, who had always been a wise woman, always told her never to run towards signs of danger. But in that moment, her body moved independently. There was something primal—she decided then—in all of us that made us want to help one another.

Miss Quinn would later say it was only curiosity and note that the late Mrs Abbott had been a very smart woman indeed.

By the time they rushed around the beach and up the stairs, the screaming had not stopped as they all had hoped, but had only become deafening, second only to the noise of the waves crashing on the shore. They came to find the source of the pain hunched over in blue at the edge of the cliff, still screaming into herself, cradling as if a child.

The others surrounding her stood in shock. Daniel and Hugo bending over the edge.

Jackie remained in her infantile state, not willing to unwrap herself or stop her cry. She seemed to Miss Quinn to look like a ball wrapped in deep blue, perhaps a big present one would receive, but Miss Quinn mind knew better than her eyes did. Even her surrounded by the blue sky and ocean, Jackie couldn't help but stand out.

"Do something! Isn't anyone going to do something!" Daniel was the first to break through the screaming. "We have to go down there! Call an ambulance."

The doctor hurried to appear, peering over the cliff as the others had done before. "I'm afraid it's too late, son. We have to call the police now."

The doctor would later say that as useless as you may be to the dead, you can always help the living, so resigned to the ill state of affairs, he instead bent down near Jackie, consoling her cries.

Eddie was the bravest of them three, to step towards the edge first. "Oh, God. Its Rebecca—"

"Eddie! what's happened?" Cecilia ran up towards them.

"No, no, don't look! Cecilia, it's Rebecca. She's jumped."

Miss Quinn edged towards the cliff—against her own and everyone else's judgement. The sky met the ocean that day and the only outlier in the view was the harsh edge of the cliff, and when looking over it, the great pool of deep crimson blood down below them.

There was Rebecca, the one member not accounted for; wearing white stained by the deep red, and with her eyes gently closed, she lay below them as her body was cradled by the rocks that killed her and washed up by the ocean that failed to save her.

The realisation dawned on them one by one that the eerie screeching noise would not be the one that followed them into their dreams that night, that instead it would be the violent crashing of the waves onto, what was, Rebecca's body.

# Chapter 4
# The Mourning Souls

The next hour or so rushed by their haunted eyes. It was always interesting, Miss Quinn noted, what toll a tragedy took from different people; some were silent amidst the chattering police and the questioning, afraid to meet anybody's eyes for fear that eerie image would follow them, because it always will follow them, they realised.

These were the people who had never seen such tragedy; who may have been surrounded by loss, but never death, and certainly never in front of them. Others cried and whined like it was their duty to mourn the dead, or to mourn the death inside of them. The child that had witnessed such a tragedy. These were the people too young to have pictured dying as an impending probability; as a corner round which they would eventually have to walk.

And then there were the people from who the toll took nothing, except the person they should mourn; the older gentlemen or doctor who had seen death as an inevitability in life, who had made their peace with it, who knew they could stand and carry on, but paused and sighed every few minutes, as if to remember that their dear friend was gone.

*What a hard job on the police,* Miss Quinn thought, to speak to grief-stricken people in the hopes of getting anything out of them. It seems by the look on his face, young Detective Carter must've thought the same thing. His stance, although, inevitably tall and lingering, betrayed his discomfort in the room. Yet like any studious British officer facing a room full of emotional people, he continued.

"Firstly, my condolences on the loss of your family. Miss Rebecca was loved by the town for as long as I can remember, and she will of course be missed. However, we still need to figure out the timeline of events this morning. I'll need to know who everyone is and where you were when they heard they scream that alerted them."

Jackie clung to her own arms as everyone looked at her expectedly, it was her who found the body after all; 'first on the scene' as they called it.

"I'm Jackie Martin," she started quietly, her voice hoarse from her cries. "My mother had worked for Miss Rebecca's family when I was a girl. I had just been visiting this past month. I had just popped outside for some fresh air before lunch. There was some rubble on the cliff, so I came closer and when I looked down, I—"

Daniel stood on the foot of the couch behind them all. He pivoted back and forth, restless more than exhausted.

"I'm Daniel Burton, I had promised my mother I would come visit so I've been here for the past couple of months. I heard the scream this morning and ran out, found Jackie on a ball on the ground."

"Where did you come from, Mr Burton?" The detective scribbled on his notepad, and Miss Quinn wiggled her nose in disdain, that noise would become incredibly aggravating she knew.

"Oh, I came from my room."

"I'm Hugo Burton. I didn't really hear the screaming at first, I was in my workshop. Did you know I have a workshop here? Yes, just past the staircase and the last door on the right! Rebecca would always say I spent too much time on it of course—"

"Mr Burton."

"Yes, of course, I was working on a new model and I heard the scream. I was afraid something happened, so I ran out and followed it." The silence resounded as he once again became quiet.

"I'm Eddie Newham. Everyone knows I've always officially lived next door, but I've been away for a while. Although, my fiancé, Cecilia, and I have been back for a few months, we're trying to remodel the house and sell it off, and go travelling. I was sailing this morning with Miss Abbott and Miss Quinn when we all heard the dreadful scream."

Miss Quinn felt it was her turn to corroborate. "Miss Abbott and I are renting Mr Newham's rooms for the summer. We arrived two nights ago."

The scribbling in his notebook was all that could be heard from Mr Carter between these introductions.

"I'm Doctor White, I've been the family physician for many decades now. I was in the dining room when I heard the scream and ran out."

"I see, and were you here on official business, Doctor?"

"Heavens, no. I was just dropping by to visit the family, that sort of thing."

"I suppose it's my turn, isn't it? I'm Cecilia Winters. I've only known everybody for a very short time, of course except for Eddie. We're getting married next May. Anyway, I was in my room when I heard this sharp screaming and rushed right over."

"And you live right over on the other side of the island, is that right?"

"Yes, with Eddie, that's right." The Detective's eyes flitted over to the officers, before he packed up his notebook.

"That's all for tonight. I'm afraid we can't do anything further before the body has been examined. Oh, and just one final question, do any of you have any idea why Mrs Burton might've jumped. Anything in her personal life perhaps?"

"I'm sorry, you think she might've jumped?" Daniel cried out.

"Miss Burton has lived on this property her entire life. She must've known how dangerous it was to get that close to the edge, and if she did fall or were even attacked, she would've tried to prevent her outcome. Some scratching or signs of resistance, or perhaps just screaming, anything to alarm someone of her situation.

"But as you've all told me tonight, the first instance of a scream you'd heard was Miss Martin's upon finding the body. And this is very important, can any of you tell me when she was seen last?"

The doctor perked up. "I suppose that must've been me. I saw her head down from the staircase. We said hello and she went promptly past me into the kitchen, where I assume she used the back door."

"And what time was that?"

"Goodness, I can hardly remember my own name these days; it must've been a little over half past eleven if they were setting out for lunch."

"And Mrs Burton was found by Miss Martin a little before noon, is that right?"

They all turned their heads as Jackie could only nod in confirmation.

Hours flooded by like this, till the silent spoke again and the weeping shed the last of their tears; till the night fell and the house was emptied and those remaining to be up fell to bed, until even the strongest of them stifled a yawn. They didn't want to admit it that night, but none of them wanted to be alone, perhaps out of fear of who they might lose the next morning. Tiredness overcame grief as they reluctantly said their goodbyes and locked their doors.

Miss Quinn was the last few to go, but eventually even she retired.

"I think I'd better head up. I'm so sorry for all your loss today, I can't even imagine."

Cecilia, ever the hostess, gave the only reply.

"You've been so kind, Miss Quinn, both of you have of course. If you'll like, I can have something sent up to your rooms for dinner? Awfully dreadful you've missed it. God, I'm not being a good hostess, am I?" She sniffled.

"Thank you, but I don't think we could stomach anything tonight." She turned to leave. "And I wouldn't worry, you're doing better than you think."

Upon barely entering her room, Miss Quinn heard a whisper of her name. To her relief, it was just Lottie, sitting on the bed with wide eyes and a worried look.

"Do you really think she jumped, Miss?"

36

Sitting down beside her, was the most relaxed she had felt all day. She decided as to what she thought. She had spent the whole day frustrated that she didn't know enough. A woman had died barely in her view, and she didn't know why! She didn't even know the woman.

"I don't know, Lottie, that's what Detective Carter seems to think, that's for sure."

"But you're not convinced, are you, Miss?"

"Something feels wrong. Why would she choose to kill herself now? And in such a violent way? And Cecilia described the screaming as 'sharp', and she was further away than we were and you could scarcely hear it! She arrived a minute after we did, how is that possible? Something tells me she wasn't where she claims she was. And, God, I don't know, but most women who kill themselves don't usually look so happy the evening before."

"About that, Miss. There's something I think you should know."

And so, before the night was over, Lottie recounted her version of events from the night before. In what some might've thought useless, Lottie knew Miss Quinn would see the poignant inconsistency. She recounted the night before, their first dinner full of laughter and stories, and for Miss Quinn turned out to be a lot of champagne.

She looked back on Cecilia's and her friend's exit into the kitchen, and as she turned her head, she caught the snippet of a conversation. One she didn't think much of at the time, and having a little champagne, didn't realise the importance of until much, much later.

As she turned back to speak to the doctor, her eyes caught a wash of navy; the taller stance of a young woman who moved to talk to an unoccupied Rebecca. A figure who bent down to her ear, and politely asked her to meet by the cliffs the next morning.

"Jackie? Jackie asked to meet Rebecca the next morning. She lied. Why on earth would she lie?"

"Yes, Miss, but what could we possibly do? We're strangers here. We can't possibly march to the police and tell them they've got it wrong."

"No, no, I suppose you're right, Lottie. We've got to be careful. I'm not sure why, but nothing seems to make sense."

# Chapter 5
# Immortality

Maybe it was the humming of the coffee or the red-rimmed eyes, but it was obvious, the next morning, to anyone who was paying attention that nobody on the breakfast table got an inch of sleep. The silence returned and those not present were assumed to be saluting the fallen. It was only Eddie who took up the burden of restoring the cheer, and the longer they all sat, the longer they realised his cheer was very unwelcome.

"Perhaps we could all go into town today, get some fresh air! Get some lunch perhaps. Miss Abbott and Miss Quinn are yet to have properly surveyed the town and we can't let them go anytime soon with such awful memories. Right, Cecilia?"

"A person has died in the house over, Eddie. Your friend. I don't think it's appropriate to be going anywhere, and I'm sure I couldn't eat a thing anyway. Excuse me." It was the clearest they had all heard her speak all morning, before she made her exit into her room.

"I probably pushed it a little too far, didn't I? I forget that she hasn't seen as much death as I…what I mean to say is, well that's not the first time a death has occurred over there, but nothing quite so shocking I must admit."

"You mean to refer to Rebecca's father…" Miss Abbott cited.

"Oh yes, old Danny boy. You know some people feel like they'll live forever. Terrible time for Rebecca of course."

A knock on the door disrupted them. A young man flashed his badge. "Detective Carter would like to see you all in the Burton residence. Now please."

Twenty minutes later, and a handful more people, all Miss Quinn could see were more red rimmed eyes. The room seemed less bright. Beyond the empty coffee cups, the chips in the banister, the stain on the table, the light flickering of the now realised chipped chandelier, all she could wonder was how she didn't notice them earlier. As was becoming his habit, the detective once again interrupted their thoughts.

"I'm sorry to say that after a thorough investigation, and primarily due to a lack of evidence, we're forced to conclude that the death is Rebecca Burton as a suicide."

A silence fell on all of them before a clear-cut voice disturbed the peace. Daniel stood on the edge of the room, finally making his way into the light. As he did, the ridges of his face became harsher; the swollen rounds of his eyes more prominent. Miss Quinn wondered if the incident has caused him to drink more.

"No, no! I don't believe it! You do a night's worth of so-called police work and think you know her! Think that she would kill herself!"

"Mr Burton—"

"Daniel, it's possible."

"No, I don't believe it! And neither do any of you. Not really. But it's easier this way, isn't it? Nicely wrapped up like the detective wants it."

"Danny!" His name was shouted once more before he stormed out.

Cecilia fidgeted in her seat. "Do you think he's right? That you've made a mistake, Detective. I mean there is the question of why she would…do it?" Everyone bowed their heads, while Eddie clasped her shoulder.

"You didn't know her as well as us, Cecilia. It's possible that some things might catch up to a person's conscience, and push them over the edge."

Jackie, whose eyes permanently seemed red rimmed and held more grief than any of her age should know, stood suddenly clutching her cup. "I think I'll go refill my coffee."

Miss Quinn stood suddenly to join her, past the drawing room into the kitchen where she met Jackie, reaching for the coffee, her hands were shaking and her grip waning. "Let me help, please."

She took the pot from her hands, as their palms touched for a moment, Miss Abbott shivered and poured Jackie her coffee. "I'm sorry, by the way, that you were the one to find her. I can't imagine how awful that must've been."

"Every time I close my eyes, it's like I see her down there again; and the waves, they keep reminding me of it. I…I can't sleep at night."

"I just can't help wondering how that could've happened to you. Why did you say, you came out that morning?"

Jackie's eyes suddenly snapped up, as did her cup. She seemed to regain her posture. "I didn't," she stated as she walked away.

By the time they got back, the detective was just leaving, and he was promptly shown to the door. While the rest of the party started dispersing, the inhabitants of the Burton residence left soon afterwards, so as not to overstay their welcome. The steps steeped as they got back to their front door.

They passed through slowly but unfortunately for Miss Quinn, she seemed to be an unwelcome visitor as her cardigan caught on the handle. Leaning her hand on the edge of the door, she didn't notice the sharp grate until it cut her and drew blood.

"Miss Quinn! You're bleeding!"

"Its fine, Lottie, it really is just a cut." She took the fabric from her top and wrapped it twice around her hand. "That should hold for a while." From the corner of her eye, Miss Quinn could spot Eddie disappearing from the edge of the room. It seemed Cecilia had already retired to her room alone.

When she found him much later, he was in the dining room with a drink in his hand and a portrait of a young boy in his sightline; a much younger Eddie Newham seemed softer around the eyes, his hunched back and much more demure appearance betrayed his present confidence. It must be time, or a great tragedy that turned him into the man he is today, she decided.

"I'm sorry, I didn't see you there."

"No, I'm sorry. I shouldn't have intruded. You look like a very happy young boy in that sketch."

"I was, I suppose. I had Rebecca to thank for it. Any time that we didn't spend being tutored or looked after, we spent together. She's the reason I am who I am today."

A photograph caught Miss Quinn's eyeline; she picked it up. A much younger Daniel stood at the edge of a cliff, perhaps in an exotic country. The shyness of his backbone was now gone, he stood with the full strength of a young man; the happiness in his eyes, she noticed, was also gone.

"That's from my travels, one of many."

"Have you travelled often?"

"Not for many years, but when I was a young man, after Old Daniel had gone, and Rebecca had married Hugo, I thought it best to travel the world; become a cultured man, as they say. Old Danny boy always said I was too demure, too meek."

"Looks like you greatly succeeded."

"Yes, well. Now to just sell this place and move on."

"Well, I'm sure the restoration will help."

"Ah, you've noticed. Cecilia thinks it will, but in my experience, this whole place is just a sinkhole. It'll keep you here; drain you even, if you let it."

"Is that what happened to Rebecca? This place drained her?"

"Trust me, as happy as she looked, she had a lot to be sad about."

"Now what would that mean?"

Eddie stood, likely to pour himself another drink.

"Nothing, you shouldn't listen to me anyway. Just get out, please, before this place takes a hold of you too."

She glanced at the little boy hanging on the wall before she left. Her hand caught on the table, and she was reminded of her pain.

# Chapter 6
# The Good Doctor White

It was noon before Miss Abbott and Miss Quinn headed for town. Her hand had bled through the flimsy piece of fabric and it seemed she appeared to be too inadequate to soothe her own wounds. They walked past the bakery, past the police station that they were tempted to drop by countless times, right into the door of the doctor.

Enclosed in a stark white building, it looked the epitome of a doctor's office. They glanced at each other in relief and entered the waiting room together. They sat in the beige chairs and took in the light of the room. There was no receptionist to be found and no other patients. Miss Quinn supposed she should feel relieved that the inhabitants of the town weren't often hurt. She began to approach the door, before she felt it crack open.

"Just give me a minute, I'm with another patient."

Instead of retreating, she leaned further. A little boy's legs were dangling off the high table, the doctor treating his elbow. Even sitting down, she could make out their conversation.

"Timmy, you have to be very careful. You could've gotten more hurt." The little boy paid no mind, sucking on his lollipop and still swinging his legs.

"Mummy said I could play outside! She had to talk to Mr Daniels."

"And where's mummy now?"

"She said I should come here. She stayed to talk to Mr Daniels, she said it was very important! But daddy wasn't there."

"Well, your parents did get married very young, Timmy, and sometimes people get older and realise they don't want the same things they did when they were younger. You know your mother and Mr Daniels get along—you know Mr Daniels is widowed, don't you, and that's alright too. You just might need to prepare your daddy. Yes, I'm sure it'll be a shock for him, but maybe it'll turn out better for everyone."

The boy, ignorant of the gossip, kept swinging his legs while the doctor kept talking about the fragility of marriage.

"Can I have another lollipop?"

"Of course, you can! If I can just find the jar…"

Two minutes later, Timmy walked out very happily with a pocket full of lollipops and a bandaged elbow, just as both the women stood coats in tow, to walk into the office.

People used to say a very long time ago, that the room of the man reflected his state, and Miss Quinn upon entry, realised, she could travel the world and never find a better example of this fact than the one in front of her.

The room she entered into was filled with mess. The desk covered in more paper than she could see wood. The medications roughly shoved into draws, the room itself was open and inviting, but the light from the window only served to lend to the frayed cabinets, full of lab coats; the patient chair which seemed to have become another storage unit for the endless papers.

"Miss Quinn! How nice to see you again! Please excuse the mess, you're not here for an emergency I hope?"

"No, no, just a small cut on my hand. I thought I'd better get it checked out. Lottie, if you don't mind waiting outside for a bit?"

Lottie, to whom such an amount of mess caused anxiety, was happy for the exit and was gone quicker than she arrived. As for Miss Quinn, she knelt her coat on the chair, found room, thankfully, and sat as the doctor uncovered her cut slowly.

"Yes, you were right to come here. The cut could've very easily gotten infected. What did you say caused it?"

"I snagged my hand on the doorframe. I was trying to run after Eddie, he seemed so upset. You see Detective Carter dropped by this morning to tell us that Rebecca's death was a suicide. You couldn't imagine how horrified everyone was."

"Ah yes, I had wondered if they heard already. I examined her body for the investigation."

"The thing is, I can't get over, well they accepted it so easily. Some cried, some feigned but nobody—well except for Daniel—actually rejected it."

"Well, we all thought young Rebecca was troubled for a while."

"Oh! I certainly find that hard to believe. She seemed like the happiest woman in the world at that dinner."

"Well, you only knew her for a day. It wasn't easy you know, her growing up in that house alone, barred from the world. If it wasn't for Eddie, I don't know how she would've survived. They grew up together very closely you know."

"Yes, I've heard, so Rebecca was sheltered?"

"Oh yes, yes. Her father was such a mean old grump, wouldn't ever let anyone near her. I had to do house calls every year just for them."

"You knew Daniel Beaumont?"

"Oh yes, very well. Didn't quite keep up with his fitness, I told him! I said Daniel if you don't get yourself together, you're not gonna be around to see that girl grow up. Oh, but he didn't take me seriously of course, only kept drinking and eating like a pig and had the gall to be surprised after his first stroke! Poor fella, he was recovering too, just before it happened."

"What a poor young girl she must have been."

"Yes, yes, and then suddenly very rich!" He belted a laugh. "You would think she'd finally travel! but she never really moved around though; only got married and settled down as quickly as she could."

"Did you know Hugo well before the wedding?"

"Oh, not so well, even now. All I know is he was an inventor who needed a lot of money for his creations. I never really thought it was a coincidence that he showed up at such a vulnerable time in her life and swept her off her feet."

"Goodness! You're not saying he used her for her money!"

"Oh no! no! How could he? On the other hand, the man hasn't invented anything worthwhile in decades! Rebecca was smarter than she seemed, I'll give you that!"

"And then came along Daniel I assume."

"Yes, young Daniel junior, they invested so much into that boy—very best boarding schools in Switzerland, France, language tutors whenever he wanted them. I think they hoped Daniel would be like the senior, and he was for a while, such a smart child. So he went to the city, and to the best boarding schools. I never really understood back then, but I think Rebecca didn't want to suffocate him; didn't want him to resent her."

"But instead, he never came back?"

His eyes shifted to her as he finished wrapping the gauze around her hand.

"They were supposed to make it up this summer, he had promised to come back."

"Did they ever make up?"

"No, no. I heard Rebecca crying a few nights before about it; seemed Daniel was desperate to get out of there again. Almost from the moment he came back, they started arguing about it. Rebecca thought she might have to cut him off for his own good."

"Wow, I wonder if he knew."

"Oh, even if he did, he never would've cared. Rebecca threatened to cut him off many times."

"Jackie's the one I really feel sorry for. It must've been so shocking to have found Rebecca like that, she's so upset still."

"Poor child. I never expected her to be so feeling. I only really remember her as a child; it's hard to properly think of her now, she was so curious! And so bright! Until the old man fell ill, she became so afraid of that house, cried every night, begged to leave, was that when he fell ill? It's hard to remember things as they were."

The light of the window hit her neatly wrapped hand, as she stood and thanked him. "My pleasure, dear, now don't you get hurt again!"

Miss Quinn exclaimed that she'd try her best as she left the old man to his work and closed the door behind her, just as Timmy's raging mother stormed, dragging her ignorant son behind her.

"You talked to him for such a long time at that dinner, what do you think of him?" Miss Quinn asked as they exited the building.

"Nice man, a little absent minded. Perhaps a little past his time to be in his profession."

"That mother in there is no doubt yelling the same thing, but it still doesn't explain why Rebecca would jump, or why everyone is so reclined to believe it. It's as if people were assuming it was inevitable, it's like all this time I've been seeing everything without actually understanding."

"Maybe she was just sad for a long time? It happens to people; you think they're the happiest you've ever met but you have no idea what's going on with them."

"If that's what happened, and the people around her really knew what the state she was in, and we have to assume they must to have taken the news so easily, then why didn't any of them try to stop her? Help her?"

"Unless they believe she deserved it? No, but that couldn't possibly be, right? They loved her! The people she had known for decades."

"And why now?"

"Well, I suppose a few things have changed. Eddie and Cecilia have come back for the first time in who knows how long; Jackie has unexpectedly come back, and now Rebecca has failed to mend her relationship with her son. Maybe it all pushed her over the edge."

"Maybe you're right, but I just can't get this image of her the night before out of head. She was smiling so wide and you could just feel how happy she was. It emanated off of her.

How could a person like that wake up the next morning and decide to kill themselves."

"Sometimes, there is no mystery, no bad guy, sometimes bad things just happen," Lottie stated as they rounded the corner preparing to board the boat back. It was evening by then. Lottie's words had stuck in her mind, after all growing up, she knew so many adults who would blame each other—even her—for the miscellaneous bad circumstances they had ended up in.

It's easier to blame a person, she knew than to just accept bad situations. Maybe that's what she had done; maybe she became like the adults, wanting desperately to find a scapegoat so she couldn't blame herself for not being there, not caring enough, not being enough to stop it.

If Rebecca had jumped, she didn't understand how she could feel this guilt, this deep gnawing inside of her, this needs to replay that night over and over again in her mind, when even the people closest to Rebecca seemed to move on so quickly. It had to all be a coincidence.

Perhaps Jackie just wanted to chat to Rebecca that morning; perhaps she had just innocently wandered out onto that cliff. But perhaps would never be enough. There is a reason behind things, and she knew as they rounded the cliff, that she would not stop until she found out why—she had to understand the life of the woman she had just met.

# Chapter 7
# The Golden Workshop

Manner was oftentimes the most important indicator of a person. Miss Quinn had always been told by her elders that upon meeting a person, it is in their gait, their voice, their presence that will tell you more about them than any of their words could. Throughout the years, this was a piece of advice that Miss Quinn found to be true.

She had seen people gather themselves standing in front of a mirror taking deep breaths, while transforming completely in the company of people, to be enigmatic and energetic; their voices raised, or lowered octaves from their natural. It was a battle between the soul of the person and how they wished to be perceived. But she had realised as a teenager that people could only pretend for so long, and God help them when their masks dropped.

So, with that in mind, it just so happened that evening that Miss Quinn could not sleep and she wandered off down to the beach and up the other set of stairs. It just so happened that the door to the Burton residence happened to be open and it just so happened that she found her way just past the staircase and the last door on the right, creaking the heavy door as she opened it.

She knew she was technically trespassing, and she knew how it would look days after a murder—suicide. It was a suicide, she kept forgetting. She wondered what those elders would think of her manner now. She decided they'd claim that no matter what time of day, or day of the year, trespassing was most unladylike. She rolled her eyes as she heard their voices in her head.

"Oh, hello!" Miss Quinn nearly shrieked as the light turned on and she was suddenly faced with a very curious face of Mr Burton and what she was sure to be a lot of consequences. She realised in that moment how hard it would be for her to describe her intrusion into another house, clad in her nightgown.

She could only stand with her eyes wide open and occasionally darting to the exit; that was until Mr Burton moved suddenly and a switch was flipped. As the whole room lit up, Miss Quinn couldn't deny the seriousness of her crime; thankfully she wouldn't need to. She could only stare in childlike wonder, her eyes widening.

*It was everything a workshop ought to be,* she thought, covered in gold and iron and solder. The light of the room made the devices come to life in front of her. She looked to step forward and accidently triggered a wire on the floor and instinctively jumped back, before she heard a 'ping!' and some distant device in the room rolled throughout.

It was a children's playground; that of course no child should ever be left unsupervised in. Mechanical toys filled the room throughout, walking on their own and clapping. Miss Quinn couldn't help but pick up a nearby bunny in her sightline.

"Oh yes! The bunny. I made those for Daniel when he was little! He used to laugh so much when he saw them, said they were his favourite thing in the world." He wiped some oil off his hands with a nearby blanket before picking one up himself.

"They're wonderful," Miss Quinn said, still in disbelief. "Why I know many parents who would give just about anything to gift their child something so inventive!"

"Oh no, no, much too dangerous!" He averted his eyes, and it occurred to Miss Quinn that he had not met them yet. "Rebecca thought they were quite something, but no. The metal, the wires, too dangerous for the little ones."

Miss Quinn smiled gently. "I'm sorry for your loss, that's what I came to say. You must've been together for so long."

Hugo bent his head down, before muttering, "Twenty-two years, nine months, and four days."

"I'm sorry?"

"How long we were together. That is our anniversary. If we're counting the day we met, then it must be twenty-four years, one month, and thirteen days." He nodded his head along with the limerick.

"That's a very long time."

"The average marriage lasts fifty-six years, so not so long." He was staring blankly onto a wall.

"But that's because she died."

"Yes." His face twitched slightly at the statement. "Rebecca jumped, that's what the police say."

"Do you believe them?" He leaned his body over a desk, fidgeting with a trinket.

"The police, they are good here. They examined the crime scene and found no trace of an assault or accident."

"Yes, but do you believe them?"

"Rebecca said she could be sad sometimes, but it always went away."

"Why was she sad?" The silence drew back at her.

"Hugo, why was she sad?"

Hugo flinched at the slight raise in voice and turned his body away completely from the intruder, reaching to cover his ears.

"I'm sorry. You know I've been all over this town and nobody seems to know a thing about you."

"I spend a lot of time in my workshop, multiple projects to work on."

"Well, who were you before you came here?"

Mr Burton stood tall, as if a child reciting a poem. "Hugo Burton, born 31 March. I grew up in a small town with my parents and was educated at Oxford before I came here. I wanted a quiet place to work on my machines. I married Rebecca Beaumont. I have a son."

"You and Daniel don't seem to be very close, if you don't mind me saying."

"Why would I mind, that seems to be a fact. We were when he was young, but then he went to so many different schools and was hardly here." Mr Burton moved around his workshop, picking up bits and pieces as he talked.

"Didn't you want to have your son around?"

Mr Burton's step faltered as he reached for a trinket. His hand clutched his heart immediately, and Miss Quinn ran to his side. He faltered into the chair next to him, breathing deeply.

"Goodness, are you alright?"

His speech faltered as well as his step. "Yes, this just happens sometimes, it's just aftershocks. I had been diagnosed with a heart murmur a few years ago, but it went away eighteen months ago."

"If you say so."

"What did you ask me? Oh yes, of course I wanted Daniel around, but Rebecca didn't want to smother him. She wanted him to grow and learn in the 'real world' she said. I just spent more time in here, I suppose."

"That must've been hard on Rebecca, being alone all the time."

"She said she didn't mind. She said she had never seen such worldly things."

Miss Quinn walked around slowly, paying attention to the walls littered with more designs and floors littered with models half finished, papers scattered on the floor and across desks, their enigmatised pairs clumping on the floor.

"It seems like you didn't get to finish all of these projects."

"Rebecca wouldn't always finance them. Creativity is good, but money seems to be better."

"Would you get to finish them now?" The man didn't answer, didn't meet her eye. She was turning to leave, fearing she really had over imposed, not that it had really ever stopped her before.

Hugo walked around to the other side of his workshop, retrieving a small plate, before bringing to face his intruder. The plate was silver with beautiful etching around the sides, and in even more beautiful writing lay a series of dates from the mid-centre of the plate. Numbers upon numbers lay carefully engraved in the metal in a spiral. She could only resignedly stare at the art. "Silver is the traditional 23$^{rd}$ anniversary gift, isn't it?"

Hugo only nodded, before pointing his oil splattered fingers on particular dates. "This is our first date, and this is when Daniel was born." Hugo could only stare at the plate. "I only ever did it for them."

She stared at the etched silver. Someone of her standing, she knew would be repulsed at the wasted material, but staring at it, all she wanted to do was to retrace each date; to know the meaning behind it, maybe to have lived through it. As she recounted the scene to Miss Abbott later that morning, she found that she couldn't fully describe the depth of his workshop, the toys, the machines.

She found she didn't have it in her to describe the sadness she felt when she looked at the silver; when she saw her own reflection and knew that Rebecca never would.

# Chapter 8
# Love and Sacrifice

It is a truth accepted to anyone who has ever been or will ever be in love, that it takes sacrifice; it takes moving your hopes and your dreams for the aspirations for another. Some people are not and will never be made for that; their own inspirations must be forefront.

Cecilia Winters had always known she was not one of those people. She knew it in the way that she moved to help others, the way affirmations and words of comfort had left her lips before she even realised. All her life, she had never been one to put herself forward, and that perhaps was her flaw. It was something Miss Quinn recognised and divulged to Miss Abbott as well soon after meeting her.

It had never crossed the latter's mind again until the day she chose to walk peacefully through town, still mulling over the escapades of Miss Quinn the earlier before, she had almost missed the glum look of Cecilia through a café window.

She wondered how a woman who in that moment could look so sad holding a cup of coffee up to her lips, could also in that moment look more polished and dressed up than anyone else there. That must be how, in her sleepless state, she recognised her; who else would wear a tee length gown to a simple town café.

Nevertheless, Miss Abbott seized her moment and wandered into the café, taking her time perusing the desserts, she decided and loudly announced on the slice of cheesecake and coffee, before she heard a voice calling her.

"Miss Abbott!" She turned to see a slightly brighter Cecilia waving her down. She walked over in comic surprise.

"Cecilia! What a surprise!" Miss Abbott came to sit opposite her.

Cecilia clasped her hands in hers, her brows frowning and lip quivering. "I'm so happy to see a familiar face."

Cecilia recoiled back, wrapping her arms around herself as they were shortly separated by the arrival of Miss Quinn's coffee and cake, which she already knew she would barely touch.

"Cecilia, what on earth is the matter?"

A child's voice replied, "You're going to think I'm so silly." She laughed nearly, wiping her face.

"Oh no, of course I won't. With everything that happened, it's normal to be upset. I mean Rebecca jumping—"

"Oh no, it's not that!" She threw her hands in frustration. "It's Eddie." She choked a cry. "He won't even speak to me, avoids me day and night, can't even look at me! And I know why!"

"You do?"

"It's because of Rebecca of course! She's died and he won't even talk to me! He's clearly in pain and we're not even close enough that he would talk to me!"

"Goodness, whatever makes you think that?"

"Rebecca and Eddie were so close, anyone could see it; they grew up together, didn't they? She was closer to him than I could ever be. Even despite the difference in our age, she knew him more than I ever could! And God, you should see them together! Cuddling in the corner, talking about old stories, their childhoods. Why any other woman would suspect him!"

"But that doesn't mean anything. They've known each other a long time. She knew him differently than you did, that doesn't make your relationship matters less."

"Then why? Why won't he talk to me? He acted like a little flustered boy around her, talked to her—really talked—in a way he never did with me." Cecilia choked back another cry as she slumped back in her chair.

"These things take time; he'll talk to you when he's ready. One of his oldest friends has just died, but that closeness you want, it takes time."

"I know, he acts like he's alright, like he can handle it but every time I try and talk about it, he just pushes me out and I don't know how to help him anymore."

"Well, wallowing in coffee and cake won't help a thing."

"I suppose, but may I tell you something? I don't really belong in this world—his world! I didn't. I don't know how to behave, if only to make him happy, if only to fit in, but it doesn't seem to be enough. I'm a fraud!" The café turned to stare at the woman in white while she cowered even more in her chair.

"You're just new here. It happens, they call it growing pains."

"It's not just that. The longer we're here, the more different he is. Quieter, detached. I think he's finally realising how beneath him I am."

"Now, don't you say a thing like that! He's lucky to have you and he'll realise it and straighten up! You'll see."

Cecilia cried into her napkin, reaching into her purse for another tissue as Miss Abbott briefly caught the flash of a lighter in her bag and wondered if she could ever recall Cecilia smoking. Then pondered that Miss Quinn would comment that given the timing of events, it might not be a bad time to start.

"And if he doesn't?" Miss Abbott drew back her gaze, quickly reminded of their conversation.

"Well then, you're just going to have to give yourself the world." Miss Abbott leaned back in her chair. She knew that Cecilia would never understand a word of what she said, but perhaps it would resonate with her; as it did for Miss Abbot, as it did for Miss Quinn.

When Miss Abbott relayed the scene for a half-asleep Miss Quinn much later, Miss Quinn commented that Cecilia had reminded her much of the girls in her town; wide-eyed, optimistic, and needlessly devoting to men who perhaps didn't deserve it.

Miss Quinn sipped her coffee, a beverage that for her was more often becoming for the evening. "So, Cecilia is devoted to Eddie but frustrated at his lack of attention and jealous of the intimacy he shared with Rebecca. If this was a murder, then that would be a pretty decent motive."

"*If* this was a murder," Lottie highlighted.

"And if it was a suicide, then where's the motive?"

"Well alright, but how could anyone have killed her? We saw half the suspects arrive to the scene, as far as we know she was alone."

"Well, you've got me there. Quick, pass me that napkin."

Lottie watched as Miss Quinn picked up a pen and drew a sharp line down the middle. "These are the two sides of the island— 'B' for Burton and 'N' for Newham. And this is Rebecca." She marked a small 'x' on the edge of the Burton residence.

"Must we use an 'x'? It's a tad morbid."

"Focus now, Lottie. I'm relying on your memory for this. Now we have to think about where everyone was and, if they would have enough time to push Rebecca and run back to their location."

"Well, we were at the beach with Eddie."

Lottie watched as Miss Quinn took aim with her pen and marked a small 'E', 'J' and 'L' on the outskirts of the Newham residence.

"Yes, and remembering that it would take maybe twenty minutes to go around the beach and back up the stairs to the Burton residence, and much more importantly, that we would have seen him coming from the beach."

"Means that he wouldn't have had enough time to go from the Newham residence to the Burton one without us seeing him."

"Exactly. In fact, I don't think anyone from the Newham household could have, which would include Cecilia, but we'll get to her."

"So, we heard the scream and ran over to the Burton house."

"Right. Now when we arrived, Hugo and Daniel were already there, they said they came from their room and workshop respectively. And we mustn't forget Jackie balled up on the ground, of course. They were all in the house. They could have come out pushed Rebecca over the edge and ran back in, only running out again when they heard the scream."

"And the doctor joined us shortly after."

"Yes, same goes for him." Miss Quinn took her pen and scribbled a small 'J', 'D' and 'H' next to the marked 'x' with a smaller 'DR'.

"And Cecilia arrived a short while after the doctor."

"And where did she come from?"

"Her room, I think that what's she said."

"No, I mean think back, where did she come from?"

Lottie closed her eyes as she tried to think back. Every scene seemed to play mute inside her head. It seemed as though the sounds of crashing waves had exhausted itself in her mind.

She thought back to what she could focus on—the dull yellow of the sand, Eddie's face as he heard the scream after her, the mass of people that eventually acclimated on the edge of the hill. She could still feel the wind becoming her towards the edge. It was when her brows furrowed that she opened her eyes.

"Why, I can't remember! She just appeared."

"Yes, remember that first night when we wondered how she arrived so quickly? We didn't see her on the stairs, and she described the scream as…God, what was it?"

"Sharp."

62

"Yes! *Sharp*. Exactly. It was only faint on the Newham residence. Something tells me she wasn't where she says she was."

"Do you think she killed her?"

"If she did, she would be relying on our panic and hazed memories to not remember where she was. She could have been at the Burton's, pushed Rebecca, ran back and then run in." Miss Quinn took her pen and marked a small 'C' in the middle of the Newham residence; a small question mark stood next to it. "Still, a lazy way to plan a murder, don't you think?"

"But if she didn't do it, why lie about being where you are?"

"Well, unless you didn't want anyone to know you where there?" Miss Quinn took to scribbling on the rest of the napkin.

"Oh, but that doesn't make much sense. They're neighbours, surely that wouldn't matter so much."

"Maybe she didn't want anyone to know why she was there. Maybe someone would mind." Miss Quinn lifted up her head slowly. "Yes, perhaps someone would mind indeed." She looked at her friend. "Do you remember what Cecilia's lighter looked like?"

"Oh, it was the ugliest little thing! Tinted old bronze with some strange carving on it. I remember thinking who on earth would want to buy that. But why does that matter?"

"I think I might know why Daniel wants to get the hell out of here so badly, and you'll never believe it! Oh, Lottie, you'll think I'm mad! But if I'm right! Oh, if I'm right, this could change everything!"

"What is it, Miss Quinn? What is it?" Lottie watched as her friend jumped out of bed.

"No time now, I've got a bar to go to, and luckily, there seems to be just one in town."

# Chapter 9
# The Misery of Man

Misery loves company. Except when Miss Quinn snuck out that night into town and found misery, where it tends to lurk. O'Neil's bar of course. She found that not only did misery detest company, but it revolted to any reach of friendship or familiarity.

She retorted that they were hardly familiar so they could not possibly be friends and the figure only stared at her, covered in the same dark suit. He held a drink in his hand, the shallows under his eyes had not lessened, instead deepened. Still, she felt sorry for the creature in front of her, to experience the loss that he had and not even be able to find an escape from it all.

Miss Quinn leaned on the bar he sat against and somewhat smugly declared, "I know why you're stuck here."

"Everyone knows why I'm stuck here, mummy dearest wanted to bond."

"Alright then. I know why you're so desperate to get out of here. So how long?"

Misery ignored her. "How long have you known Cecilia?"

He turned to her with the most mocking expression. "Why, only a few months, Miss Quinn."

"How about we skip the part where you deny knowing her, and I get you to confess?"

"Confess to what?"

"To killing your mother."

"What—"

"You wanted out of here desperately and she kept you here for months against your wishes, suspending your money and restraining any attempt to leave—"

"That doesn't mean I killed her. My God, you have a dark imagination."

"Then what happened? Truthfully."

"It was around a year ago, last summer I had been vacationing at a friend's house."

"And you started your affair."

"No, no, it wasn't like that. We had gotten to know each other. I started to care about her, that's all."

"I saw you run out of your own house multiple times; how about you try being honest. So, do you love her?"

Finally, a man stared back at her, with strained eyes and a strained response. "I can't."

They stared silent at each other.

"You know, people say time slows down when it happens, but it doesn't. It speeds up; it speeds up till you can't catch a second; till you can't breathe and keep praying to live it over and over again, to get that one moment back."

"How did you meet her?" He leaned back in his chair and sniffed turning away from Miss Quinn.

"God, does it matter? She was a friend of a friend or something stupid, and I didn't realise then." He paused tentatively. "I knew her for months and months. We had gone to the seaside, to the café almost every day, we journeyed back and forth."

He breathed a beat before continuing.

"One day we had spent together, just one day, I remember the sun was so bright, I thought I could barely see." He smiled sadly.

"We were talking—just talking—well, maybe arguing and I said something stupid. I don't remember what. She was sitting across from me, and she just laughed and smiled. God, just this big smile. And I knew. I knew that I would love her more than I can imagine. Maybe I was already in love, and I was too much of a fool to realise, but in that moment, it hit me like this intense wave of bliss, invincibility, and warmth.

"It felt like I could do anything, and nothing else mattered, and that everything would always be ok, because of this moment. This moment where she smiled at me and suddenly everything was perfect. I didn't immediately realise what had changed, but I knew something happened to me that second."

He looked up with pain in his eyes.

"They say that you feel tied to someone you love, I didn't. It was scarier than that. It was like there was this person who could do anything to you, who could love or hate you, but you would still willingly tie yourself to them, because as long as they were happy, so were you." He smiled wide. "God, I was smiling like an idiot for hours after that and I didn't even know what was wrong with me."

"But she didn't love you back." It was then that he turned to her.

"No, she doesn't, and happy perfect moments can only last so long, right? But seeing her then, knowing her for months, knowing everything she wanted—I wanted that so badly for her, even if it wasn't with me. I couldn't give her everything she needed. I'm a mess, I could never take care of her like she deserved."

"Don't you think you should have at least given her a choice?"

"I was never a choice."

Silence, in a bar, could never befall anyone, but in that moment, it did.

"And then Eddie."

"Fucking Uncle Eddie. I didn't know she was here; I swear I didn't."

"It's unfortunate."

"It's life's fucking cruel joke. It's enough to know that she's happy, but to see it every day, and you can't even leave. Or say hello, or make sure she's ok."

"But you did. Make sure she was ok, that is."

"The morning she died."

"I wondered how it was possible that Cecilia heard the scream better that I could, given she was in the Newham residence. But she wasn't, was she?"

"She was with me."

"Why didn't you just tell everyone, the whole truth?"

"Cecilia didn't want anyone to know her status. Last summer, she was there as a maid, not a guest. And besides, Uncle Eddie could be jealous, possessive, and she just wanted to make him happy."

"And you just wanted to leave."

"I couldn't. I already told you that."

"So, you did what you had to?"

"You think I killed her. God, of course, that's why you're here."

"Well, did you?"

"I'd have sooner ended up on the rocks of that beach. So, no. I didn't push my mother off that cliff."

"You think she was killed?"

"I think it would take a hell of a lot for the police in this town to do a damn thing."

"I would've thought a potential murder to be enough." She brushed her fingers over her silken gloves.

Misery stared again at her; it was the first time she saw his hand leave his glass.

"My mother didn't just fall. She knew the danger and she never would have stood that close to the edge."

"And if she jumped?"

"Why would she?" His hands threw in the air. "She was perfectly content and happy—"

"As far as you know, your father worked on his inventions, you weren't there, your Uncle Eddie has just come back. Maybe it was loneliness."

"No, no, she wouldn't. I'm telling you, I don't believe it!"

"Well, why would someone kill her either?"

"I don't know, I don't know."

"Think, Daniel!"

"Trust me when I say I tried to be around as little as possible."

"You're drinking in a bar on a Tuesday. I believe you." Miss Quinn finally sat down next to him, her hand on her chin.

She didn't see him lean back in his chair. "Except I think you left someone off your list."

"Jackie. Of course, but why would she come back after all these years? Never mind wait months just to kill your mother?"

"All I know is suddenly she showed up after all these years and somebody ends up dead. And let's not forget, she was the first one there. Coincidences like that never happen."

Miss Quinn looked up at him. "Almost never."

She grabbed her jacket and walked away from her chair.

"Miss Quinn!" She turned to face the man.

"How did you know about me and Cecilia?"

"Your lighter, Daniel. I don't think I've ever seen such a horrid thing in my life, and I doubt anyone would ever let a duplicate be made."

# Chapter 10
# Death and Funerals

Charlotte Abbot was a precocious but uncurious child. Even though she grew up in poverty and hardship, she had always been told to look for the silver lining around any cloud. And eventually, as she grew older, the precociousness drifted out of her, and she became simply uncurious.

She often thought about how she described herself in negatives; she wasn't unkind, uncaring, but even as she grew and accumulated a generous pay and an un-boring life, she felt as though she still lacked. It was perhaps because of her lacking that Miss Abbott lived a simple but wonderful life; full of warmth and life, true friends and happiness.

Miss Quinn's mother too, she knew, had an intolerance for questions and the impatience to explain the logic. The difference became that Miss Julia Quinn, daughter of the very wealthy Mr and Mrs Jack Quinn, instead became stubborn. She would push the boundaries of what she knew, because she wanted to know everything.

What Miss Abbott didn't realise is that, walking back from that godawful bar, Miss Quinn never wished more that she was like her friend. She wished she could stop thinking, could stop wondering. She knew it made her unlikable; she knew her crass and blunt words were taken as hurtful, as signs of her unhappiness; not that she ever really considered herself to be unhappy.

Miss Quinn considered herself to be suspended, in a space between a happy childlike entity and like misery itself. She knew she was simply content, for all her living, she had never really felt. She didn't mean to make those around her unhappy, she just didn't know how to be anything but herself. She often feared that who she was, was an extremely intolerable person.

Miss Quinn also knew that as much a person could try, they could never change their essence, their being. Even if they never really knew what was, fitting in would only cause you to lose yourself. She had known that a long time before she reached the steps of the Newham estate.

The sun was just rising from its cradle. She hurried in quickly not wanting to face the obvious fact that she had stayed out all night again. Quickly, she returned to her much younger state, tip-toeing around the manor, her fingertips grazing the banister. In another reality on another night, her father would have caught her, and sent her to her room nevertheless; he was never really good with punishments.

Her shoes were hanging on her other hand as she crept towards her room, and nearly fell from her hand when she saw her friend simply sitting on her bed with a cup of tea in her hand and a book in the other, as though nothing in the world was wrong. She was almost scared to disturb her. Luckily, she didn't have to break the trance.

"Miss Quinn! You're back."

"Yes, but what on earth are you doing up so late?"

"Oh, never mind about that now. What did you find out?" Miss Abbott surprised herself; perhaps she hadn't quite lost all of her curiosity after all.

"Daniel claims he didn't push his mother."

"Daniel? What would his motive be?"

"Cecilia and Daniel met last year. When you mentioned the lighter, I had realised I saw Daniel with it. And when we were all questioned, I couldn't quite place it then, but someone called out for him when he ran off."

"Danny."

"Exactly. We had spent the past evening talking about nothing but him, and I had never heard anyone call him that, not once."

"You think they had an affair?"

"Goodness, no. Cecilia is much too devoted to Eddie, but Daniel is clearly in love with her and wanted desperately to get out. Only his mother holds the purse strings."

"She does as well for Hugo."

"Yes. But Daniel has been going around saying his mother's been murdered. Why would he do that if he was the one who killed her?"

"To frame someone maybe?"

"I don't know, it still isn't making sense. There's still one person we have to talk to. Jackie lied about why she was there in the first place, and we still haven't figured out why. That is when it began, I'm sure. I'm so sure, Lottie, that if we only figure this one thing out, everything else will unravel. I just don't know how; Jackie has hardly been seen since it all happened."

"I think you're forgetting something, Miss, tonight is the funeral. She's bound to show her face."

"You're right. But we should probably be well rested for such an event, so right to bed."

"But it's already dawn. For how long, Miss?"

"Why, until the event of course!"

It is at this point, important to note, that nobody saw or heard of Miss Quinn until the much later evening, when she came down in what Miss Abbott might have described to be glamorous for a funeral, but she knew better than to have that conversation; at least it was black, she shrugged. Miss Quinn straightened the bow on her dress before she approached her friend.

"Lottie, goodness, I was expecting more people. If I knew it was the usual suspects, I wouldn't have dressed up so much."

"Shh! Miss Quinn, you can't say that, the family might be offended."

"Given the size of this house versus the few amounts of people in it, I wouldn't worry so much," she stated as she picked up two champagne glasses from a passing waiter, extending one out to Miss Abbott.

"Come on, they'll surely toast to Rebecca at some point, and we wouldn't want to be rude, would we?"

Miss Quinn skimmed a little of her champagne as Miss Abbott haphazardly took hers. Miss Abbott scanned the room. She had been there at least for an hour before her friend made her entrance. Out of the modest amount of people that had walked by in mourning, there was nothing she could do but stare at the portrait of Rebecca by the entrance of her door.

She didn't think it was a very recent one; something about the haircut maybe was different; but it certainly showed her well. Her oval face covered delicately by her flowing dark hair, the squints around her eyes as she smiled; she must've been a happy person. She decided to think that Rebecca lived a happy life.

She didn't hear Miss Quinn's ramblings, nor did she hear the door when it opened, and she was only alerted to the presence of Cecilia when she had obstructed her view of the deceased, and she remembered the fact that this woman's life had ended.

Cecilia had stood at the altar of the door, looking worse than she reckoned she ever did before. Her eyes were too fixed on the portrait, her hands grasping her handkerchief.

Miss Abbott approached her carefully tilting towards the coveted picture, she didn't say anything. She didn't know what to say.

Cecilia finally noticed her presence next to her. Pulling back her tears, she said, "Miss Abbott." It seemed Cecilia didn't know what to say either.

"I'm sorry not to see Eddie with you," Miss Abbott offered.

"I just don't know what I'm doing wrong. He won't talk to me and when he does, well, he's relentlessly cheerful, like nothing at all has happened." Cecilia looked her in the eyes, as Miss Quinn moved to join the conversation.

Cecilia once again looked down at her hankie. "This is his, you know. I walked into his room just to see him and he was staring out of the window, so I started to cry, and I saw this on his desk and just snatched it up and left."

It was then Miss Abbott realised that she and Miss Quinn were not mourners, they wouldn't dwell in this world. It might be a part of their lives, but it will never become part of their person. They were passengers, travellers. They had almost let themselves forget how gruelling grief can be, so they remained as voyagers for the funeral; they were outsiders.

Though Miss Quinn wondered if in their world, anyone was ever really an insider. Perhaps Rebecca was, once upon a time, and maybe Daniel could've been, and Cecilia certainly wanted to be, almost it, even. It had struck her again how different interpretation can be from reality. She realised she really knew nothing.

Miss Abbott moved around the room, watching people coming in and out; some still crying, some still shocked. Miss Quinn remained on the outskirts, with champagne in her hand. She leaned back on the walls, where she knew nobody would notice her. Eddie entered after Cecilia had, and he, for the first time they had seen him, seemed like he had seen sorrow. Pain was in his eyes, although he had them cast so far downwards, anyone would barely notice.

He moved purposefully through the living room, past his beloved fiancé, fixated himself onto the casket in the front of the room that nobody else had dared to approach. They watched as he pulled his hand upwards, hovering above the casket. The gloss of the finish reflected the shadow of his hand, and he watched it, before pulling his hand back. They all again watched as he left the room but didn't dare follow him.

It was Hugo who approached the casket next. He stumbled around before finding his footing. He touched the casket with both his hands, and knelt his hand upon it. Nobody would recall how long he stayed like that, unmoving from her. It wasn't until his son stood behind him and grasped his shoulder, that Hugo looked up from arms, only to go back to the room. Still Daniel stood grasping his shoulder, faint tears in his eyes.

Miss Quinn couldn't watch the scene; she averted her eyes and when that didn't drown out the cries, she excused herself the porch. She leaned against the building, wondering what she was missing inside it. As it turned out, she wouldn't have to wonder for long as the doctor approached the top of the stairs.

"Goodness, those never get easier, do they?"

"I wouldn't know, remember?"

"Yes, of course. How is it in there?"

"I would prepare yourself."

"Perhaps it's better not to go in at all."

Miss Quinn sprung from her stead and twirled her arm around the doctors. "Ah, but we must, to honour her memory."

They walked past the threshold, only to see Jackie at the foot of the stairs, her red tinted eyes pointed at the casket. Her face was trembling as much as her hands. It seemed to Miss Quinn to be a wonder that she was still on her feet, after all nobody had seen much of her after the funeral. The doctor noticed Miss Quinn's inquiring eye.

"You know, it's a shame. I think Eddie and Miss Jackie must be the only people left who knew Rebecca from before."

"Before?" Miss Quinn turned to her chaperone.

"I only mean younger, I suppose. Before everything, when old Mr Beaumont was still alive. Except for me of course, but I barely count."

"Why is that?"

77

"I was never really here. Rebecca, her father, Eddie and even Miss Jackie as a child, all lived here together, just before everything seemed to get so…"

"Complicated?"

"Yes. Perhaps things were always complicated."

Miss Quinn thanked her chaperone before excusing herself; she walked straight into the living room, straight to Miss Abbott.

"That missing piece we were talking about," she whispered. "I think it's time we talk to Jackie."

They both stared towards the young woman by the foot of the stairs as she shook her head and tears ran down her cheeks once again. Cecilia moved to comfort her, but her help was pushed away before her cries once again enveloped the walls of the house.

She shook her head harder and pushed Cecilia forcefully across the room as she shook on her feet. "You don't understand! You all don't understand! It's my fault!"

The room stared after her as she ran away, while Miss Quinn leaned over to Miss Abbott. "And I think we'd better do it soon."

# Chapter 11
# The Woman in the Coat

Jackie Elizabeth Martin had always felt echoes of emotion. All her life, it was snippets running past her. She knew she should be feeling more; she should be more effected by the events of her life, and perhaps it was a coping mechanism manufactured by a childhood of loss and endurance. But she just couldn't catch it, the intensity that everyone else seemed to feel.

All her life she was stuck with whispers of emotion. She replayed them over and over in her head often, just to feel anything.

That was until the morning of Rebecca Burton's death. She had almost been relieved to know that she was capable of feeling so deeply. And once the emotions started, they couldn't be stopped. They had lived on the brink of her eyes all her life and now she feared she would never be done spilling them out. She would have made fun of most children crying as she did now.

As she ran outside, her tears echoed in the dark skies, embalming themselves in the winds, drowning the ocean. She perched on a cold stone bench as she wept. She knew she would never understand why she felt such deep pain for a woman who she's barely known.

What she had known was that Rebecca had been immensely kind to her, and that thought alone made her cry harder until she couldn't even hear the steps of those approaching her; not until she felt a hand on her shoulder and Miss Abbott's eyes looked back at her. She lifted her high onto the bench. Miss Quinn, who she now realised was behind her, made some remark about how that was better than being beneath it.

"I don't understand, why are you here?" The young woman shuddered in the cold.

Miss Quinn lowered herself down. "Jackie, we know you were going to meet Rebecca that morning. We know you lied, what we don't know is why."

"Why! Why does it matter now?"

"Because the time you arranged to meet her, she was already dead. Don't you think her family deserves to know why?"

"It was my fault, alright! Mine! I made her do it!"

Miss Abbott reached out to comfort her. "Jackie—"

"No! You don't understand! None of you do! It was my fault; she might be ok if only I hadn't brought it up! If only I hadn't made her remember!"

"Remember what? Jackie, you're bumbling." Miss Quinn shook her.

"I remembered! She didn't think I would, but I did!"

"Start from the beginning, child!"

The woman sitting in front of them slowed her breathing. The panic stopped but the shaking still remained. They watched as she closed her eyes and lowered her voice.

"I was only a child when my mother worked for her that is. I was so young and small and curious that I would sneak around, and nobody would take notice of me. I would sneak into the kitchen for sweets anytime I liked; I would hide behind curtains until everyone was gone and then explore this house for hours. Then Mr Beaumont had his first heart attack."

"Rebecca's father?" Miss Abbott leaned in closer.

The young woman nodded and continued, "After that, my mother became the nurse too, and we started living here. I was so happy at first. I didn't get on with other children and never had much interest in making friends. I was just happy to explore and snoop."

She lowered her eyes to the ground. "But it wasn't his first heart attack that was the problem; it was his second. It practically immobilised him; he couldn't move, he couldn't speak very much, he would spend entire weeks in bed. Rebecca came to his side instantly, but his condition wavered from better to much worse, until no doctor could predict if he was going to remain well.

"All of summer that year he was recovering, getting stronger and stronger, and Rebecca became more fused to him. She would take him on walks to regain his strength; she would read his favourite novels to him. She barely left his side. Until the end of that summer, he died suddenly. His doctors had just assumed his condition had worsened again. He was a man with a severe heart condition, it wasn't out of the realm of possibility for them that it just stopped."

Miss Quinn looked down at her. "Just assumed?" She stepped forward slightly. "So, what really happened?"

The young lady on the bench started crying again. Her face covering her hands, until Miss Abbott placed a gentle hand on her arm. "We can't help you if you don't tell us."

She lowered her guard, sniffling. "It was the night before his death. I was playing hide and seek with my mother. I was hiding behind the curtain on the landing of the stairs, just below his room. Rebecca had just left to meet Eddie over on their side of the house for the evening, but I saw her figure come back up.

"She was wearing this long dark coat. She didn't see me but I saw her shadow enter her father's room. I was curious, she was supposed to be at dinner already. So, I crept up to the door; her back was facing me and I saw her take her father's hand and whisper something in his ear. And then…then she took a pillow from beside him…"

Tears streamed Jackie's cheeks as she struggled to carry on. Her fingers gripping her knees. She was no longer hiding from the truth. "She took the pillow and placed it over his face. His whole body struggled until he went limp. I didn't understand what I saw until perhaps a year ago."

Miss Quinn pushed, "What happened, Jackie?"

"Her figure turned, I think I must've made a creak on the floorboards, so I ran away and never told anyone what I saw."

"This wasn't just a visit, was it? Why did you come here?"

Her eyes formed harder than both women had ever seen them in their short encounters. They saw a peek of the strength of the woman before. "That memory tormented me for decades. It played over and over in my head without me even ever realising. It is the reason I can't sleep at night; it was the reason I failed out of the school, the reason I have been in therapy for years.

"It ruined my life. You will never understand that. So yeah, I came back because she owed me! Owed me for everything that my screwed-up life turned out to be. I figured that if I dropped enough hints, she would understand; that she would pay me to live well for the rest of my life."

"You've been here for months. Dear God, how long does it take to blackmail someone?"

"It's not blackmail!"

"My mistake. Extortion?"

"It was penance."

"It was greedy," Miss Quinn retorted.

"It was no use. She just kept ignoring me and brushing me off. So, I had enough. I arranged to meet her that morning to tell her what I knew explicitly, then she would have to give me the money. That's why she jumped."

"Because she was faced with the reality of what she'd done."

"She couldn't ignore it anymore. Not with me about to expose her. The guilt must've been too much and she…she jumped. If only I hadn't come here, she'd still be alive. I'm the reason she's dead."

"Why wouldn't we believe you're the one who pushed her?"

"What?"

"Let me paint a different picture. You had spent your entire life angry at Rebecca for having ruined your life, so you come here for money. But when she refuses to give in, you arrange to confront her about her murder, but instead in a fit of rage, you push her over the edge. You can't believe what you've done, so you think fast!

"You run back into the house and then leave again, making sure the doctor sees you leave, and then you scream before you even reach the end, so everyone rushes out and nobody even questions you."

"No! no, you have to believe me, I'm telling the truth. I swear ok, I know what I did. I know I blackmailed her, causing her to jump, but I didn't push her of that cliff."

Miss Abbott and Miss Quinn only looked at each other in what could be described as hesitance.

Miss Abbott comforted the young girl after they had brought her back inside, and both women watched her slinking in the corner. Miss Quinn leaned back on the grand wall of the Burton Estate, perusing the bereft. Hugo was nowhere in sight, and it seemed young Daniel was finally reluctant to leave his mother as he gripped the coffin.

The only person in the room who seemed unconcerned with their own grief was Cecilia, as she sat with her body facing Eddie's as he held his head in his hands; it seemed grief caught up to everyone.

"Why aren't you happy?"

Miss Quinn refused to take her eyes off the scene, afraid it would change. "I'm afraid you're going to have to be more specific, Lottie."

Miss Abbott looked to her side before whispering carefully, "When everyone else was convinced she'd jumped, you wanted to know why. I would have thought now that you know, you'd be beaming for joy."

"Well, that would be rather inappropriate at a funeral."

Miss Abbott gave her a look that Miss Quinn was convinced she must've learnt from her own mother.

"Oh, alright. Maybe I was hoping this woman had led a more interesting life; maybe I wanted to believe there was something more to it, that she didn't choose to end it."

"Well. Now that we know she did, and why. Do you think we ought to tell the police?"

"Oh, what would be the point? Both the victim and the murderer are dead anyway. Some might say justice has been served."

"I don't think I like your mindset."

"But you can't tell me I'm wrong."

The pause gave way to silence, before the doctor had approached them. "Ladies, we're having a little toast in remembrance of Rebecca."

"Oh goodness, our glasses! We've completely forgotten!"

"No need to worry, Miss Abbott, Eddie is fetching new ones. Rebecca's favourite he said."

Just on cue, Eddie entered holding a tray of the most intricate champagne flutes Miss Abbott was sure she'd ever seen, which held what we guessed to be the most expensive champagne she'd ever taste. She watched as he, again with a smile on his face, slowly extended his hand to pass everyone a delicate flute.

"Miss Abbott, Miss Quinn. I know you both didn't know Rebecca for very long, but I do hope you'll join us."

"Of course." Miss Quinn reluctantly let go of the wall supporting her, until she stood at the centre of the room, joined by the others around her.

Eddie started, "We haven't done eulogies around here for thankfully a long time, so I suppose all I can say is…well, I know the people Rebecca loved most are in this room and I know she's thankful we're all together." He raised his glass to her, staring into the crown, preparing to drink, before Daniel interrupted him.

"I just wanted to say, well that I'm sorry I've been a nightmare to deal with this summer. I know my mother wouldn't be proud. I was just so reluctant to believe that she'd jumped because I thought I knew everything about her, and it kills me because the reality is that I tried my best to always be away from here, so how I could possibly know everything? But I'm going to try to be better now. I'm going to try to make her proud."

He raised his glass with a small smile as everyone downed their drink. Miss Quinn hated to admit it but perhaps her holiday was coming to an end. She didn't realise then how young the night really was.

Jackie watched the room as everyone sipped their drink while she downed hers. She had known all along that what she had done to Rebecca was terrible. She knew she was a terrible person who became nearly as bad as a murderess. She knew she would spend the rest of the night wondering how she could live with herself.

Even so, this felt better than being as hollow as she once thought herself to be. It was with that thought that she said her goodbyes and preceded to sleep, blissfully unaware of her hand still clutching the delicate intricate champagne glass.

Miss Abbott and Miss Quinn watched as the party dissipated and the solemn guests relinquished their champagne flutes, one by one, going to sit around the living room. Miss Quinn never could handle silence very well.

"What was she like?"

The room turned to face her as if she had done an abhorrent thing; it might have been too early to speak of the dead.

"Well, it's just that like you say, Lottie, and I only knew her for one night so I just wondered what was she like?"

It was Eddie who spoke quickly. "She was happy; she was a pleasantly happy person. She had this glow about her which seemed to make her infallible. She was also a dreamer; a naïve girl perhaps."

"It's hard to know who a person is," Daniel followed. "It's not evil or good, or nice and unpleasant that draws the line. It's the intricacies of a person that makes them who they are. It was in her smile, her laugh, composure that was her essence. In that regard, I'm sorry, but I don't think you'll ever really know her."

"I'm sure you're right."

Eddie fumbled with his glass. "Oh! It seems we've got a glass missing!"

"I think I saw Jackie take hers upstairs," Cecilia piped up.

"I think I'll go retrieve it quickly."

"Oh, Eddie, don't! You'll wake up the poor girl."

"I'm sure she's not asleep by now."

"Oh, alright, but I'll go with you."

The scream came not much later.

# Part Two

# Chapter 12
# The Second Suicide

It was when the inspector visited the house for the second time, and they all began to reflect on what happened, they realised they weren't at all sure what had transpired. Each of them remembered a frenzy; a mass of hysteria as the scream alerted them to the danger; as Cecilia flew down the stairs and they realised they could barely remember what she said.

As they, followed by the doctor, ran up the stairs and came to find a scene in which Jackie was laid by the armchair, surrounded by the smallest white pills blending into the carpet and the prized champagne flute rolling back and forth on the floor. They do remember that it was the doctor who stepped forward to check the pulse while Eddie stood back to give him space.

They remembered the panicked look on his face, his confusion, failed resuscitation, and subsequent despair was theirs as well. They remembered the ambulance arriving, but nobody could quite recall who made that call.

"That's what seems to happen in panic, people don't seem to quite remember things," the detective noted.

One by one, they all realised that, despite every window in the house being closed that night, all they could hear was the crashing of the waves on the shore. They came to realise it was the only fragment piece of their memory that would stick with them. They also came to terms with the realisation that another member of their house was gone. Dear sweet Jackie couldn't be saved.

"I am again deeply sorry for your loss. Jackie's suicide, I—"

"I'm sorry, did you say suicide? Two people have died here in less than three weeks, and you think this is some big accident?"

"I'm sorry, I shouldn't have said that so soon, but the evidence does seem to suggest this is another suicide. You all did say that Miss Martin was agitated at the funeral. That she went up alone and that Miss Winters and Mr Newham proceeded to find her upstairs, not breathing. And there is the amount of sleeping pills scattered on the floor."

"So that it? You've found something that fits just fine, and you refuse to look elsewhere?"

"Like I said, Miss Quinn, there is no evidence t—"

"Yes, I'm well aware of what you said. But it is my understanding that the police don't just usually wait around for evidence to find them."

A beat paused.

"In such suspicious and surprising circumstances, should you not at least conduct and autopsy? Or test her glass for poison?"

"I'm sorry. But it seems there's nothing else we can do."

With that, the inspector took his briefcase and team and walked out after the ambulance, and the house felt yet another loss, and a little more silence. None of them dared to speak yet. Miss Abbott knew Miss Quinn was puzzling it all together in her head, but she herself was filled with guilt. She already knew the story, and Miss Quinn refused to let her tell anyone.

She knew that a young Miss Rebecca Beaumont killed her father, been blackmailed by her desperate friend and had jumped out of guilt. She knew that once the police had figured that bit out, it was only a hop-skip and jump to Jackie feeling so guilty that she too killed herself.

Miss Abbott was almost sure her friend was thinking the exact same thing, but seeing it completely differently. She had known Miss Quinn for long enough to know she would never be satisfied with a half answer.

The grief took its toll differently this time around. Those who at first cried, seemed to have run out of tears, so they instead became silent. Those who at first succumbed to silence, felt that they had paid their penance and dared to speak. And those who had already found their voice, dared to move, to once again have autonomy in their lives.

They watched as Miss Jackie Martin's body was carried out of the house. It seemed to strike Miss Quinn as odd in that moment. How differently she would be remembered by everyone standing round her. Eddie would remember her as a young girl. She knew Miss Lottie would remember her as reckless and dangerous. She would only remember her as the girl who led a life half lived.

Everyone wants to stay young, but she was not yet old enough to tell the stories of her life. Her life had been ended without any toll—'had been ended'.

Miss Abbott and Miss Quinn took their exit down the stairs as she thought about her own mistake—'had been ended'. It was pretty clear what had happened. Of course,

Jackie had blackmailed Rebecca and Rebecca, in her guilt, took her own life. That was the motive they were looking for, and they had found it.

So why did she insist on the detective running more tests, insist on Lottie keeping quiet, insist that the young life of Jackie Martin 'had been ended'. She walked side by side with Lottie down the narrow stairs, while Cecilia and Eddie lingered behind them. They had all been resigned to the fact, even unknowing of the motive, that these were a series of tragic coincidences.

But as Miss Quinn walked down the stairs, she felt it nagging at her brain, pulling at her tongue, appearing and dissipating in front of her eyes. She was missing something.

It was with this thought that Miss Quinn's heel scarcely missed the edge of the step and she fell backward; lucky that all three people reached to grab her before she came tumbling down the stairs.

"I'm alright, I'm alright," she assured them as she stood herself up and flapped the dust off her skirt, even though it was much too dark to see. She considered for a moment, as she continued her decline, how on earth Eddie could have run down these stairs that morning. No wonder he looked so flushed.

She regained the image of him one of those few first times; eyes wide, forehead already sweaty from the heat and tucking his handkerchief back into his pocket as he elegantly ran down the stairs like a madman. But she was wrong! It wasn't these stairs he was climbing down that morning; how could they be? No, it was his own very identical set of stairs. Goodness, what a nuisance that high wall is; it's a wonder they haven't broken through it by now anyway.

She looked to her friend, hoping, but ultimately knowing she would not be thinking the same thing. Lottie had barely said a word after anything, and it wasn't until they became settled in their room that they both sat on their beds, resigned a sigh and spoke again.

"It's my fault," Miss Abbott spat out ashamed.

"Now don't you go perpetuating this cycle! It most certainly is not."

"But I knew, Jackie told us! And I did nothing. Maybe if I spoke up, told somebody then she wouldn't—"

"Who on earth could you have told? The inspectors on the mainland, you couldn't have reached him, you know that. And I'm the one who told you not to, so if anything, the fault is with me!"

Lottie paused for a moment, keeping her gaze on her lap. "Are we really not going to tell them?"

"No, not for now, Lottie. I'm so close! I know I am!"

"Not one of your hunches could explain how anyone killed them, Miss. I mean how did they do it?"

"For Rebecca's…" She hesitated to say murder, knowing she would be fought against. "Accident. The only people we could really rule out are you, me and Eddie. Oh, and Daniel and Cecilia; he said they were together at the time."

"So that's how she heard the scream."

"So that leaves everyone in the Burton household; being the doctor, Hugo, Jackie and exempting Daniel."

"We know about Jackie; she claims she didn't push Rebecca because she wouldn't get paid."

"I believe her, she seems logical. I mean, would you really stay here for so long and lose your temper the moment you're going to get what you want? No, that doesn't seem right."

"Alright, well what about Hugo and the dear doctor?"

"All I know about the Hugo is that he's presumably inherited his wife's estate. I saw his workshop and, well, he'll finally have the money to finish his inventions. But we know next to nothing about the doctor."

"Well, alright, but what about Jackie's death?"

"Well, that's where you come in. I need you to tell me everything as you remember it."

"But why! Surely you have your own recollection."

"Yes, yes, of course. But maybe you saw something I didn't. And I don't want to influence your version of events by telling you mine."

Lottie's brows furrowed. "But won't mine be an influence on yours?"

"Undoubtably, but considering how quickly I drank my champagne, you may be of more help."

Miss Abbott noticeably struggled not to roll her eyes as she cast them upwards and tried to remember the events. "Well, we were all sitting on the couch when Eddie noticed one of the glasses was missing, so he went upstairs, with Cecilia as she got annoyed at him to get it back.

"Then we all heard that dreadful scream and Cecilia ran frantically down the stairs, stared at all of us in shock for a good minute before blurting out 'she's not breathing'. So, we all followed her to Jackie's room."

"See, that's the bit I don't understand. The rest of us were gathered in the living room, we would have assumed that the trouble was in Jackie's, so why bother running down to tell us. But I shouldn't be interrupting you, Lottie. I'm sorry, dear, go on."

"Well, we ran into the room, doctor first of course. And you must remember Jackie laid out on her armchair, her head thrown back like that, and we couldn't see her chest rise. And, Julia, you know I tried so hard not to look at her face. It all scared me, so I looked elsewhere."

"Yes, and what did you see? Be very specific, Lottie, this could be important."

"Well, I focused my eyes down, you know how I do when I get nervous? The carpet was this pale pink. I'm not partial to it honestly, but that's why I didn't notice the tiny pills around her armchair at first but then I realised how many there were."

"Yes, yes. And that's when you nudged my shoulder to show me."

"And I yelled it to the doctor. And he started chest compressions, but her pulse wouldn't come back."

"Yes, that's right. Where was everyone? Do you remember?"

"Yes, that was pretty clear. Everyone was by the door frame watching; the doctor was with Jackie of course; Eddie was knelt by the armchair and Cecilia had just crumpled down to the wall on the side of us. Does that tell us anything?"

"Maybe, I just can't quite see it yet."

A pause grew between them as both women readied themselves for bed until Miss Abbott suddenly sprang. "Oh! And the glass of course. So stupid to think of now. It was to the right of Jackie's chair rolling back and forth on the floor."

And with that, the lights were shut off and both women were promptly asleep.

# Chapter 13
# The Matter of the Money

Due to the simply impertinent nature of the ending of Rebecca's funeral, her will reading, which had not all been properly scheduled, was promptly moved to the following day; not even tragedy could stop inheritance. The messenger of Rebecca's final wishes came in the form of a stout older man carrying a briefcase larger than his desire, or indeed qualifications to stay in his business.

A thing that came apparent when he greeted them in Burton's living room with a sigh and unwavering deep-set eyes which expressed no desire to be there.

"I think you all know why I'm here." His modest clothes somewhat undercut his tone. His aged appearance which should be a sign of wisdom, instead spoke of inexperience. The only thing of value around about him seemed to be the document in his hand, which became much more obvious as everyone leaned in at its sight.

Miss Quinn rolled her eyes. Of course, she had no stake in this game, she couldn't possibly after knowing the woman for an evening, and she hardly reckoned anything terribly surprising would happen. The truth was most will readings seemed to be the dullest affairs. She sighed; she would never commit her loved ones to such a dull affair.

She noted that unless you were the person expecting to receive a substantial inheritance, the whole thing seemed to pass you by. Although, even Daniel seemed unfazed as he leaned back in his chair struggling, much like his father, to keep his head straight with that of the lawyer.

Herself and Miss Abbott, rather expectantly, leaned back on the walls at the back of the room, like children who hoped their parents might make the mistake of forgetting they're there and let them stay up longer. It felt rebellious, intimate, she realised, to be standing in a space occupied by her dearest family as if she was somehow arrogant enough to believe she might inherit something.

The mockery of a day continued as she watched the lawyer pull out the tiniest spectacles which she aptly thought was relative to this size, but she knew commenting on it would only start a fuss, and even she could realise this was not an appropriate time for her remarks.

"Firstly, to the matter of the estate; it is Miss Burton's wishes that Beaumont house be passed over to her husband, Hugo Burton," gesturing his hand over the front of the room as if a child was lost. "And then she explicitly stated that upon the death on Hugo Burton, the house reverts back to her son, Daniel Burton."

Daniel and Hugo, who sat at the front, seemed to shrink in the recognition; their stature staggering but no surprise befalling on their faces.

Miss Abbott leaned over to Miss Quinn. "I wonder why Rebecca didn't leave the house straight to Daniel, isn't that odd?"

"Yes, I suppose most wives must be scared of their wealthy widowed husbands remarrying, and their subsequent replacement. But I don't think that's a worry she would have about Hugo, besides the house reverts back to him."

"Yes, well, I hope he takes care of it." Miss Quinn knew what her friend was thinking; she assumed that just because Daniel seemed to have made a mess of his life that he'll make a mess of everything he touches. As she glanced around the room, she knew people were sharing the same thought. She could have sworn she heard the word 'unfit'. She sympathised, the same assumption was made about her, once.

"And now on to her liquidised assets." They watched as the stout short man took some papers from his worn satchel. "Now, this is rather more complicated. Hugo and Daniel Burton will of course inherit the majority; however, Hugo will remain the overseer of Daniel's trust where the majority of his money lies; until, and I'm quoting here, 'Daniel presents himself sound and capable enough to take upon himself the responsibilities of the house, according to Hugo Burton'.

"Or of course, in the event of the death of Hugo Burton." The word 'death' was exaggerated rather too much for the liking of everyone in the room, as most looked down and winced. Even the hypothetical thought of a long-sighted death suddenly became too much for them.

"There also seems to be a small fund set up for Mr Edward Newham, it seems Rebecca wanted to show her gratitude for all those years of friendship."

Eddie, for once, seemed to be on the side-lines of the group. He sat on a chair in the far-left corner and simply hung his head down. Miss Quinn realised she had never quite seen him in pain. Cecilia, who was almost always by his side, instead, at this moment stood, on the right side of the room scrunching her shoulders.

"And it seems that she was also keen on leaving the good doctor a considerable amount for his practice."

Miss Quinn could've sworn she heard the lawyer comment that hopefully the money will go to good use to a cleaning service; it seemed she wasn't the only one distraught by the doctors' 'messy' hospitable practices.

They all watched expectedly as the lawyer flipped through the papers until he reached the end. "Well, it seems that wasn't so complicated after all." He packed his bag and showed himself to the door. As he started whistling, he said his final goodbyes. "I am sorry for Rebecca; it came as quite a shock to me. I'm also sorry I happened to miss the funeral. I hadn't even seen her for years. God, what a shame it all is."

And just like that Miss Quinn realised the most interesting thing about the will reading happened to be the lawyer himself.

It was much later, when Miss Quinn was sat in the bed in her room, that she noticed one thought popping in her head over and over again; why on earth would a woman filled with guilt, who perhaps knew that she was close to taking her own life, not pay one last visit to her lawyer? Although, perhaps she was overthinking things, yes that must be it.

It was just as highly probable that Rebecca's suicide was spur of the moment upon discovering her secret might be revealed, which led to the guilt of Jackie over the blackmail she must've caused leading her to in turn take her own life. Yes, that was the story, that makes sense.

What Miss Quinn didn't know, was that someone else was repeating that same narrative to themselves at that very moment, thinking 'yes that makes sense' and 'yes they must've believed it'. Whether it was the person steadily holding a drink in their hands, the person holding a smile or the person shakily applying lipstick staring in the mirror or any multitude of others, she wouldn't uncover until much later.

# Chapter 14
# The Story of Jackie

Miss Quinn had never quit a thing in her life—unless it irrevocably bored her—but Miss Abbott knew that as Miss Quinn sauntered around biting her tongue and averting her eyes, that she wouldn't last much longer. She had tried to repress herself once, not say the most inappropriate remarks possible; a situation that ended with her bursting her opinion on everyone at Jenny Linnen's ninth birthday party.

She didn't like how some girls were treating the birthday girl and said some 'unkind words' which were reported back to her parents. Needless to say, her attitude never made her very popular. But it was at that point in her life, that Miss Abbott had learnt a lesson as she watched Miss Quinn's parents try to reprimand her—people don't change, not really at least.

But regardless of the past, Miss Abbot found herself unexpectedly unnerved by the silence of her friend, and with silence comes a lot of time to overthink and lying in bed. That night, Miss Abbott found herself twiddling the ends of her sheets, filled with doubt. What if Miss Quinn was actually right?

After all, it was her who came to her friend with doubt of Jackie's story, and they had investigated the best they could, never mind that Jackie's death had no sign of suspicion on it. Although, they had never looked, they seemed to be no way of checking; the police department took all the evidence and told them nothing.

Miss Abbott looked to her left; her friend was still soundly sleeping, and she knew how much she would hate to be woken. She pulled the covers out from under her and slipped on her nightgown and shoes as she tiptoed out of the room. She grabbed a box of matches, Eddie's presumably as she walked out the front door and used one every few minutes as she lit her way down the long stairs.

Luckily, it was still the tip of summer and the air remained humid. She walked across the side of the beach mentally timing herself as she did so, her mind drifting back to the morning of Rebecca's murder. 'Murder'; why on earth did she say murder? It was a suicide; everyone knows that by now. She couldn't have possibly been murdered, and who on earth would want to kill her anyway?

She was a wealthy woman, much smarter she suspected, than anyone ever gave her credit for. But was money really a motive? With her death, Hugo would get the finances to finish his machines and Daniel would get the freedom he always explicitly hoped for, but nobody else would benefit, would they?

Her feet reached the bottom of the stairs up to the Burton residence and she started walking up the rickety stairs. Her hands now becoming familiar with the matches. She supposed that Cecilia could've felt some envy at the closeness between Rebecca and Eddie, but to push her? And Eddie! Oh, that's right, he had inherited something, a small amount of money from Rebecca to show her gratitude for their 'years of friendship'. Oh, but he had looked so upset when it was announced; how could he have possibly done it.

She placed her hand on the cold doorknob and pushed her way in. Miss Quinn would roll her eyes at the idea that two 'accidents' had happened and still nobody had locked their doors. It was with that thought she walked into the open living area and stood in the middle of the opposing couches, reliving that day.

They were all sitting down, the couches splitting between them on the day of the funeral. Jackie had just downed her glass of champagne and disappeared upstairs; everyone had surrendered a word of sorrow before Eddie twirled his glass and realised one was missing; that was the moment he went up and found Jackie dead. Surrounded by her white pills, her pills.

Miss Abbott lit another match as she creaked carefully up the stairs to Jackie's room. She was lucky that it seemed distant from the other rooms, at least she wouldn't wake them up. She carefully turned the doorknob, lighting another match as she went in. She didn't know what she hoped to find as she neared the couch at the corner of the room.

She remembered Jackie's lanky body laying back on it. It seemed pale and dark in her mind now; she drew closer and stared at the floor beneath it.

The last time she saw it, it was white with pills. The detective's notes repeated in her head over and over again that Jackie dies of an overdose. Lottie supposed if she really believed that, she would be sound asleep in her bed by now.

A chill came over her. This may be the room a murder took place, but this was definitely the room a young girl died.

That was something Miss Quinn failed to consider, that these were real people who lead full real lives, not just puzzles for her to solve. She considered Jackie as she walked around the room; what she knew about her, what she could tell. She remembered her somewhat distinct clothing, in all shades of blue; her harsh eyes and her harsh tone.

She considered that first dinner; only now realising it was Jackie who brought Old Daniel up in conversation as she traced the edges of the bed Jackie would've lied on. She recalled the dark shadows under her eyes when she first met her; perhaps slept not so well then.

Her hand rested on the cool knob of Jackie's dresser. She wanted so desperately to open it, to know her better, if even slightly. Miss Abbott knew Jackie's deepest secret, her darkest nightmare, and still found herself irrevocably falling into the unknown. She pushed it open, only slightly, only enough to later claim it wasn't her fault, in that coy manner only she could.

The rustling inside startled her. The police combed through this place, there wasn't supposed to be a single speck of dust, left alone what she found to be an empty pill bottle. It rolled to the edge and cooled her fingertips. Questions flooded her mind; questions she would've once chastised Miss Quinn for. What was the prescription for? Where did Jackie get it from? Is this what she overdosed on?

She clung to the bottle now. She didn't know why she came here, but she knew she found what she was looking for. The tiny white pills cascaded in her mind. How many of them were there scattered on the floor? Ten; twenty? She climbed down the stairs and back up again. She wouldn't let go of the bottle until she reached her room, and safely set it on her dresser.

She wasn't sure when she woke up that morning, what she had done in her hazy dream, but she saw her muddy slippers and the bottom of her best gown drawn with dirt, and most importantly, a bright orange bottle facing her.

It was that morning when the shame of what she had done had faded away and been replaced with curiosity…that she peered closer at the bottle on her desk, close enough to observe what previously had been too dark to see. She noted the prescription of the highest strength sleeping pills, and almost fell out bed to wake Miss Quinn when she noticed who had prescribed them.

# Chapter 15
# Heartaches

There was something about death. Miss Quinn realised as she reached the doctor's office early that next morning accompanied by her friend. There seemed to be a distinction between those who could handle the loss and those who couldn't. As a doctor, she realised he must be well acquainted; after all, it was his medication that killed a patient, and he barely batted an eyelash.

She nevertheless expected to see him at least bent over his desk in deep emotional pain, but then Miss Quinn did always tend to be a tad hyperbolic. No, instead she found him clearing his study, a thing perhaps more surprising.

She cleared her throat, waiting for him to turn and when he did, she saw no indication of distress; no hollow darkness under his eyes, no thin pursed lips, nothing but the seemingly transparent demeanour he always had on. She clasped the orange pill bottle under her hand and lifted it, placing it upon his desk before he could speak.

She was done with pretending, the false of it all, the grandeur of a mystery and the excitement of secrets. People around her either kept dying or breaking down.

His face fell when he looked into her eyes, and then Miss Abbott's. Something had changed between them all. It all became too real, too hard to deal with. It left them all in silence.

"I can explain," he blurted.

"Please do." She sat down in the seat like any other patient would.

"Miss Martin—Jackie had trouble sleeping. Ever since she came back here, she was plagued with anxiety and nightmares."

"So, you prescribed her something."

"I couldn't do anything, I'm a doctor. I'm supposed to help people, and she was suffering."

"But you didn't just prescribe her anything." She grasped them back in her hand. "I know these. You prescribed her the strongest sleeping drugs, ones that can only be prescribed with the recommendation of a psychiatrist."

"She insisted mild medication won't help at all. I was inclined to trust her."

"How could you possibly have prescribed them alone?"

"I have a psychiatrist friend of mine, known him for years; it wasn't hard to…sign his signature."

It was Miss Abbott who had a great respect for law, who in that moment was astonished. "How could you be so irresponsible?"

"Irresponsible? Young lady, I have been the doctor of this town for decades. I've watched everyone grow from their christenings to their funerals and I trust my patients. You have no right to tell me how to conduct my practice!"

Miss Quinn stood up swiftly. "She does when your medication kills your patient! That's what she overdosed on that night, isn't it? Those were the little white pills. Did Jackie know how dangerous they were? No, I bet she didn't. I bet you didn't even bother to explain it to her. Maybe if you did, she would still be alive."

"Jackie overdosed by choice, that was clear in the autopsy."

"If you were the one doing the autopsy, then I don't trust it. And besides, we'll never know that, thanks to you. Who else knew she was taking the pills?"

"It's hard to say. I mean they were all living in the same house, any one of them could have stumbled on it—"

The good doctors' eyes went wide, and he paused before continuing.

"It possible that—that I may have chatted to Jackie about her medication over for dinner at the Burtons'. Only a few times! But it's possible that anyone may have overheard."

"You discussed her private medical records with her outside your practice." Miss Abbott, who in most arguments found herself reserved, couldn't hold back.

"I was her doctor; I knew what was necessary."

Miss Abbott fumed. "You skipped procedure for your benefit."

It was at this point, Miss Quinn finally felt the need to step in.

"And what about Hugo? When did he start regressing?"

The doctor turned on his heel, leaning his hands on his desk, facing his own silence.

"How did you know?"

"Healthy people don't tend to bend over in pain."

"It only came back recently! You must understand that. Hugo comes back every couple of months for a check-up, especially for his heart—"

Miss Abbott jumped in. "And let me guess, you have a nice chat with him and send him on his merry way."

"I didn't think it would ever come back! It's been years."

"But it did, didn't it?"

"It's been a decade." He finally turned back around. "I caught it only a few months ago."

"Did Rebecca know?"

"She came to see me a couple weeks ago. She'd noticed the change in Hugo. He didn't want her to know you see. She blamed me for not catching it sooner. She said I had grown too comfortable in my position and become incompetent."

"You know, I bet anything she threatened to take away that handsome pile of money in her will."

"She threatened to ruin my entire practice. Can you even believe that? A girl I've known since she was so young, any doctor could have made that mistake."

"So, she threatened to ruin you, you get so mad and push her off that cliff before she has the chance?"

"No! I could never." Shock filled his face.

"You really expect us to believe that your whole life was at risk, and you did nothing?"

"Oh, Rebecca never would have done it. She's just some silly girl with more money that she can handle!"

"Was. She's dead now, remember?"

It was then that both women walked out of that office, with a determination to find the truth and the escalating need to check the credentials of their current doctors.

It was on the walk back that they really dealt with the repercussions of what they now knew.

Miss Abbott fidgeted with the edge of her top. "So, Hugo had no real reason to kill his wife because he knew he inevitably would be dead soon, is that right?"

Miss Quinn slowed down at the sidewalk; her brows furrowed, and her head hung. "It doesn't matter, it was a suicide; they both were. We stirred up memories of Jackie's trauma and she felt so guilty she took her own life. Sometimes there is no mystery, sometimes we are the monsters."

"But hypothetically, stay with me. Hugo didn't kill his wife for the money, he wouldn't have it very long anyway. But the doctor, the doctor knew after he was confronted by Rebecca that she would cut him out of the will. The money he had always been promised would be gone. That might be a reason to kill."

"Alright, I suppose the doctor was at the Burton residence, but he arrived after Hugo and Daniel, and they have no reason to protect him."

"Alright. Well, what about Daniel? He wanted desperately to leave but Rebecca wouldn't let him! What if he pushed her and Hugo protected him!"

"Lottie, Lottie, nobody even knew Rebecca was going to be there, except you, Jackie and Rebecca herself. Discounting you as a suspect, Jackie felt so guilty she killed herself, and besides, Daniel was an advocate for the murder of his mother from the off. Why on earth would he steer the investigation away from a suicide if he was the one who did it?"

Lottie's face dropped. "I don't know how to explain it. It's like suddenly the whole story doesn't make sense to me."

"I know what you mean, but every turn we take leads us back to a suicide and the same problem over and over again. Rebecca was the only one on that cliff."

That was the last thing Miss Quinn said as they took a small boat back to the island. Nevertheless, one word hung over and over, indenting itself in her mind—'Story'. The whole story didn't make sense. She tried to tell it to herself over and over again, eventually realising she was trying to convince herself of its truth.

She nudged that inquisitive feeling in her head back, and back, until it became a faint echo. A word she couldn't quite see before her eyes; a word she didn't remember on the tip of her tongue.

It was in this state she found herself still walking up to the Newham estate, only a faint cry from the upstairs bedroom knocked her out of her thoughts. It reminded her of that dreadful morning when everything started, of Jackie hunched over like a child.

They had found Cecilia like that, hunched over her vanity in pain, clutching the handkerchief she seemed to be so fond off. Her eyes were wide and pearled as she finally looked back at her gently crouched on her bed.

"Is it about Eddie?"

"No, no, it's not about Edward."

"Daniel then."

Her eyes grew impossibly wide as she flinched, and her eyes flitted to the firmly shut door. "You know," she whispered.

Miss Quinn could only nod. She thought it best to say as little as possible in the event she messes up. She wished Miss Abbott was here.

She dabbed her eyes as she cried harder. "It didn't seem so serious at the time. You have to understand that I never meant to get so hurt. It was just an accident; it was just a big accident." She shook her head.

"You know my station, I was working there, and I'd see him every now and then. We exchanged a few words, and our eyes would linger a little longer than usual. I think now that we were fascinated by each other."

She paused greatly.

"Then one day, in town, it was raining so heavily and I…was barely getting home. I had my flimsy jacket over my head." She laughed slightly.

"And he just rides up in his car and offers me a ride; he makes some joke about the weather and smiles. I rush in breathily heavily, stuffing myself in that car shamelessly, but he doesn't mind, acts like I was sitting there all along, and simply gives me a ride back. Silly, isn't it? How simply things can start."

Miss Quinn failed to respond.

"After that, I see him in town and I wave and he waves back. I feel my heart jump a little but that's all. Then we talk more and wave, and talk, and before you know it, we start walking into town together. He's funny, nobody expects that, but he is. He challenges me and I challenge him back. I think then, that's why I like him. We goad each other on every day like kids.

"The silliest things: the name of a bottle I mispronounce, some board game I claim is useless, anything to keep us talking longer than a minute. There became this friendship between us, these hidden meanings, these little jokes I'd hold onto every day.

"And before you know it, it's like this big lingering dare between us; this silence filled with everything we're not saying, and how close can we get to it before actually breaking it? We play with our words in every argument. They get quite complicated, our arguments that is; quite hard to keep track of. It becomes a game of who can keep it up the longest? Or who slips up first, reveals something they shouldn't."

"Their feelings?"

She smiles sadly. "Yes, I suppose so."

"So, what happened?"

"It goes on for months and months. And then, it's like one day he wakes up and decides he doesn't want to play anymore; just like that he can't even look at me. I think he's finally realised I'm beneath him, and then there's wall between us. That's when I realised how much I actually missed him. Miss him. Anyway, I couldn't stay on after that, I left not much longer after he did."

"Are you in love with him?" As soon as she'd said it, Miss Quinn wished she could take it back.

Cecilia only looked back and tensed, holding back more tears.

"You never mean to fall in love, you know? There's this one moment in every relationship I think, where you know you should turn back, that this is the tip of the iceberg and that if you keep going you could fall in love; you could get hurt, maybe both. But nobody ever turns back because it's too fun and exhilarating to have that light in your life.

"Because you don't want to go back to your old, life, mostly because you don't see the harm in it, I think. I didn't turn back. Trust me when I say, I laid my own bed."

"What about Eddie?"

"Darling Eddie, I do love him."

"Not like Daniel."

"Never like Daniel."

"God knows what Eddie would think if he ever found out. He's known Daniel all his life. How cruel the world is? It got better when I met Eddie, that ache in my heart; and it gets torn back open every minute I see Daniel again. Every time I remember what we had, what we could've been. How he tossed me aside.

"I thought it would get better, that if the love went away so would the pain. But the love never went away. I'm resigned to the fact that I love him irreversibly and irrevocably, for the rest of my life."

"You act as if it's a death sentence."

"A part of me has been dying ever since I met him, because I know he could never love me back. Because I know that's something I have to live with. If he had broken my heart, that might've been one thing, but it's not broken; and I have a terrible feeling it's going to spend the rest of my life suspended waiting for him."

# Chapter 16
# Revelations

Miss Quinn had never left well enough alone, and packing to leave that next morning, she realised she simply didn't know how to. She had caught Miss Abbott glancing at her every now and then. She was still of the mind that they should extend their stay and see how things play out.

Miss Quinn, on the other hand, realised she had already seen enough tragedy for one holiday, and that they should leave swiftly before the autumn leaves started to fall.

So, their goodbyes were swiftly said, and they exited the door with their luggage. Miss Quinn assumed Lottie was as sad as she was to remember their holiday in such a tragic way; to remember the faces of their hosts as haunted and darkened. Miss Quinn later thought that it must be one of life's greatest miseries to know how to fix something but be unable to touch it.

They both moved unbearably slowly through the house and down the rickety stairs, both knowing the other was remembering that singular morning, feeling naïve knowing what they knew now. It was when they sat their luggage on the small boat, that they came to terms with the fact that they would never really know what happened on that small drifting rock.

Except for the story, the papers came out this morning, everyone knew the story by now. Miss Burton—formerly Beaumont—had jumped off a cliff from her estate on the morning of 11 June 1934; her son to inherit the majority of her assets. Except that, nobody but them knew why.

And then a week later at her funeral, Jackie overdosed on the sleeping pills irresponsibly prescribed to her by the doctor. Nobody but them really questioned the reasoning behind that either. They didn't suppose anyone ever would again.

It rang over and over in her head. Rebecca killed her father. Jackie blackmailed her, Rebecca jumped, and Jackie overdosed. The trajectory of one death caused another. And then another. Still, she remembered Rebecca's face the night before, holding a small glass of wine, smiling to Daniel sitting next to her. She supposed initial impressions could be wrong.

As they reached the mainland, Miss Quinn turned to Miss Abbott. "I think we have one more stop to make before we head off."

Together, in silence, they walked along the road to the police station; criminals about to confess their sins, or perhaps believers going into confession. They would have to accept that this is as much of the story as they would know, but keeping that knowledge to themselves is not a privilege they could live with. Not when Daniel deserved to know why his mother jumped, or when Jackie's family deserved to know the root of her illness.

Their breaths grew shallower as they reached the door, and everything around them became silent. What should have been a bustling police station—for a small town at least—

faded into the background as they reached the desk of Detective Carter.

They sat down without pretence, without introduction and told their story—and with hesitance—the story of many others involved. They relived their arrival and the descent of many others around them. They didn't lie per se—Miss Abbott frowned upon lying but they felt it important to leave out certain details so they forgot to mention instances of Daniel's acquaintance of Cecilia, or Hugo's heart attacks or the doctor's sloppiness.

In their defence, they weren't aware of how much they would stumble upon when they started their little escapade for the truth. All they wanted was a motive to understand how a woman whose life was complete, could turn out to be so hollow. They ended up getting answers for questions they weren't even sure they wanted.

Looking back, staring into the hollow eyes of the detective while he scribbled in his notepad as they confessed their sins, they were almost sure they wanted it to happen, that 'eureka!' moment that would make everything make sense; perhaps a premeditated gasp might draw out an epiphany. They sat there for hours, until they became sure they missed their train; until their throats dried up and they had to close their eyes for moments at a time just to recount the story.

They pictured the scenery, the murders—the accidents over and over and over—until they didn't even remember why they started this little journey. There was no justice that could be done for Rebecca now, she was dead, and Jackie's guilt over it led to her suicide. They remembered walking up those first few steps just a couple weeks ago.

Everything seemed different now. Everything was so distant from its initial impression. Cecilia and Daniel were heartbroken; Rebecca would be cast as a murderer, so desperate for her freedom that she killed her dying father, but not so desperate that she—

Miss Quinn stood up abruptly, her eyes widened. "We must go! Now, we have to go now!"

"Go where? What's happened?"

"Oh, Lottie, I've figured it out. There's still a murderer in that house! And I know who it is."

The detective interjected. "But there's no murderer. They were all accidents you just said so yourself!"

"I think that's what we were made to think! Now, quickly, grab your coats. We have to go to the bar; we have to see Daniel."

An hour later, when the sun had set and the family had settled into dinner and polite conversation, not without a few missing seats of course, Daniel Burton once again stormed into the dining hall and dived straight for the whisky. Nearly making this a habit, he borrowed a clean glass off the table and rang it with a knife, not that he actually needed the extra help to grab everyone's attention, as dinner at this point had ceased in his presence.

"Son, why don't you sit down and eat with all of us."

"There's no need to miss me. I've decided to stay."

"That's great news!" Eddie said.

"You didn't let me finish. I'm going to stay until I prove who killed my mother. I know she didn't jump off that ledge and unlike the rest, I refuse to believe that story. She lived to see me grow and get married and start a family, she wouldn't just leave us."

"Son, perhaps—"

"And there's something else. I know which one of you killed her too and I'm not going to stop until you're rotting in jail for your crimes."

And with that statement, the prodigal son ran off. Nobody even bothering to notice that he didn't even pour a drop of the whisky. It was much later that night of course, that the fruits of that little speech would unveil themselves.

Much later that night, when an uninvited guest creeped into the Burton Estate, walking purposefully past the living room, grabbing a throw cushion on the edge of the couch where they were always so perfectly placed. The perpetrator sweated, worrying their leather shoes would squeak against the wooden floorboards and give them away in this pin drop quiet room.

The fire roared and lit up the dark room, bringing out the emerald green of the armchair facing it, as the intruder carefully gripped their gun and held it against the plush cushion, ready to disturb the smoking gentlemen laying on the armchair. They were worried they would cough on the smoke, why did Daniel have that awful habit anyway?

They could see it tomorrow—Daniel found by his father, said to have enjoyed one last smoke before blowing his brains out, red splattered all over the emerald green, mahogany study Rebecca worked so hard to decorate. It was then that they brought up their gun. Finally, everything would be over. They paused, taking a deep breath as they always did, before cocking the gun.

They had to choose the angle of the gunshot carefully. Remember, a right-handed man can't have shot himself on the left side; they had to think.

But before they could, a bright light shined in their eyes, disturbing them before they were tackled to the ground. They squinted before opening up their face, and stood in front of them was Miss Quinn, Miss Abbott and Detective Carter. He knelt before them, his hands caught up and tied at the wrists and straight ahead.

In the reflection placed on that side of the wall, Eddie Newham squinted before staring at his own face. The sudden bright light still bothering him and the gun he held now in the hands of the detective.

# Chapter 17
# The Man in the Coat

It was just before dusk when Eddie Newman broke his silence. Miss Quinn understood then he had been taking the last hour to rehearse his way out his predicament, but relying on your charm and likability can only take you so far, especially when you were caught with a gun in your hand. He sat on the armchair, the near scene of Daniel's final resting place.

The emerald green of the walls which once lit up this study instead became imposing and Daniel gripped his head tighter, staring at the ground.

His fiancé, a generous word to use at this time, stood at the window of the room, the furthest away from him; while Daniel shook with rage by the armchair, the others simply observers.

"Why? Why did you do it, Eddie?"

The accused man simply didn't move until Daniel shook him. "Answer me! You were our family and you killed her! Why?"

"He doesn't have to answer. I know he did it. I know why and how." She paused before looking at Eddie, his head still frowned. "Are you going to tell them, or shall I?" When no reply was heard she continued, "Alright then."

Everyone paused as Miss Quinn started.

"Consider two things—the untimely deaths of Rebecca Burton and Jackie Martin. That was the only cause and effect we saw. Rebecca killed herself and Jackie killed herself too. It's not until you ask why Jackie felt so guilty, why she came here when she did that you understand what really happened, until you understand the third cause and effect.

"Imagine a young girl running around this very house, perhaps nearly twenty years back. A girl who got so bored in such a big house, who sneaked around and played hide and seek. Now imagine one day, hiding behind a curtain, she sees something she wasn't supposed to. She witnesses the murder of the master of the house.

"She sees someone sneak up the stairs into Old Daniel Burton's room, the summer he was on bed rest. She sees someone put a pillow over his head and suffocate him. But she's just a child, she doesn't understand what she's seeing but she's scared enough to begin hating this house and blocking the memory for decades.

"And then twenty years later, Jackie Martin, with depression and no life prospects, relives the memory and finally understands what she saw that day. She comes back here thinking she might as well make some quick money; thinking she's owed it after everything she's been through."

"But Jackie never asked us for any money, and she was here for weeks," Hugo piped up.

"No, she doesn't. Because she accuses the wrong person, and because she been doing it so subtly, nobody even notices it. Remember that dinner we all had together? Remember now often Daniel came up? Now do you remember who brought him up?"

"Well, Jackie I suppose," the doctor chips in.

"If I had to make a guess, Old Daniel must've been talked about a lot recently. Jackie doesn't say it outright, she only alludes to how suddenly the death was, hoping Rebecca would get the hint."

"Are you saying my mother murdered my grandfather?" Daniel fidgets standing up.

"I'm getting there. So, Jackie spends the whole month bringing up Daniel again and again and again, and Rebecca doesn't get the hint, why? Because she didn't do it!"

"I don't believe he was murdered! I'm the one who did the report!" The doctor piped up.

"And that's why, it was so easy to get away it. This was a man already on his deathbed with multiple heart attacks. You can't honestly say you questioned it," Lottie countered and the doctor's brows furrowed.

"But how do you know it wasn't Rebecca?" Cecilia countered.

"Because why would she? Why would a woman kill her already dying father? And then name her son after him as a constant reminder of her sins, or why would she supposedly be desperate to leave this place, and the minute she can, stay here for the rest of her life?"

"Then who did it! Who killed him?" Cecilia piped up from the corner, afraid to ask the question.

"I realised from the moment we came that the only person who had ever insinuated that Rebecca was trapped and so desperate to leave was Eddie. It was him of course." Miss Quinn turns to him. "You did it, didn't you?"

"But why?" Cecilia argued.

"We're getting there I promise. So, Jackie witnesses who she thinks is Rebecca murdering her father, only its Eddie. So, she spends a month accusing the wrong person and getting nowhere. But back to that dinner party, at this point, Jackie gets frustrated. She wants her money, so to hell with subtlety.

"She corners Rebecca at that dinner party and asks her to meet her on the hill that next morning, something that Miss Abbott overhears—"

"So, Jackie killed Rebecca and then herself," the doctor interluded.

"No, now, listen more closely. It occurred to me much later that if Miss Abbott overheard then, there was a good chance someone did too, namely Eddie who was sitting on the other side of Rebecca. Now, before this point, Daniel presumably being the only person in the room getting Jackie's hints, must have thought they were harmless, that she's bound to go away at some point and never come back; but when he overhears them, he understands one of two things can happen.

"Either Jackie talks to Rebecca and Jackie figures out she genuinely has no idea what she's talking about, and figures out Eddie is the only other person who could possibly be the murderer, or Rebecca finds out that her father was murdered, and again, Eddie is the only other person who could've done it. Neither revelation working out too well for him."

Miss Quinn turns to Eddie. "I can't imagine dealing with what you had to for a lifetime; that burden, that anchor, but it's time to set the truth free, because to understand the next part of the story, you have to understand the fact that Eddie spent his whole life deeply in love with Rebecca."

She continued with less jovial spirit then she had before. "See when I first came here, all I heard was that they 'grew up together' and that 'they were so close', but I thought how could that be with a literal massive wall separating them. You want to know what I think? I think Old Daniel never liked you, never liked you in his house, or for his daughter.

"He thought that you were an uncharacteristic unambitious coward who hung around his daughter, and I can only imagine that resentment in you building for twenty years. Now, I don't know where it is, but I can picture the two of you as young kids breaking a little hole in the fence and sneaking through either side. It was only wood, even kids could find something heavy enough to break that.

"So, against Old Daniel's wishes, you grew up with her anyway, fell in love with her, anyway. Until twenty years later, all that was left between the two of you was an already dying man. But you said it yourself, he was resilient and wouldn't let go for anything. He certainly wouldn't give you his blessing, would he?"

"No," Eddie whispered, his head still in his hands.

"But you loved her so much, you wanted to set her free. You thought if only that old bastard would just die. You wanted to save her. You were her hero, and then grief would take over and she'd lean on you, and then you would get married and live happily ever after. She would never know the awful things you'd done.

"So, you crawled up those stairs, maybe intending to kill him, maybe you wanted to talk to him. God, I bet you'd spent your life trying to grow into the man he wanted for his only daughter, but he didn't respect you anyway, did he? He saw through your little act and maybe he'd put you down for the last time, and before you know, he ended up with a pillow over his head."

Miss Quinn leaned down in front of him.

"But she didn't love you back, did she? You weren't the hero in her story, and even through I'm sure she didn't know of the terrible thing you'd done, you two grew apart anyway. And she met Hugo and had a family, and a little boy called Daniel. Maybe that was your breaking point. You couldn't stand his ghost judging you all over again. So, you left and you didn't come back."

"You don't understand, I had to come back." His face finally lifted from his hands.

"For the property, I'm sure. You know I stayed in your house for weeks seeing endless changes that Cecilia made, but not a single one of yours. But God, you must've been surprised to see Jackie back here sprouting every little thing about Old Daniel she could remember. I mean, God, what a welcome back! Welcome home, you committed a murder!"

"I had no other choice!"

"You had every choice! And when you pictured Jackie and Rebecca talking on that hill, you panicked. I bet your life flashed before your eyes. Everything you had worked so hard to become—successful, wealthy, you came back here with a fiancé! Finally, your life was becoming good; you were on the brink of the happiest years of your life; a fresh start away from this place! And it was all about to be taken away from you."

"I didn't mean to—"

"Don't you dare say that. You woke up the next morning with every intent to kill someone. We'll never know if you meant to kill Jackie or Rebecca, but my guess is that once you got on that hill and you saw Rebecca standing there, all you saw was the girl that rejected you when you were young. The girl you loved your whole life who wouldn't even give you the time of day. I think you saw red and took your handkerchief out of your front pocket and you pushed her."

It was at that point that Eddie paused and stood up.

He stared at them; with an expression they will later say they never recognised on him. They realised they had only ever seen him smile, even on the brink of tragedy. They would shrug and say it was his disposition to be cheerful, to see the silver lining in everything; they never understood why until that moment.

"You have no idea what it's like," he started. "To love somebody with your whole self who does not love you back. To know it so strongly in your heart that this person standing in front you is the only person you'll love for the rest of your life. That you found the greatest love of yourself at such a young age, and you'll never find anything like it.

"To live and die at such a young age that you don't care what the rest of your life looks like; to go through the rest of your life knowing you will never, ever find that in another person. To be in love before you even know what love is; to have it grow inside you and consume every action, thought or word before you even understand why. I blamed her; I knew that.

"And Hugo came along, and I was so resentful. I just kept thinking if I'd done one thing differently, she would be with me instead of him. I knew I would always love her, but I couldn't stand around and watch while she loved someone else."

"And that morning on the hill?"

"I heard Jackie asking Rebecca to meet. I could see how frustrated she was becoming, and I knew it could only be about one thing." He paused before finally looking up at his witnesses. "I had to stop it. So that morning, I snuck off early. I knew I had to be quick—"

"You had me and Miss Abbott to use as an alibi of course."

"I snuck through the hole in the fence we made years ago. I barely fit through, but I made it just to the clearing on the hill. I saw Rebecca and muffled her mouth with my handkerchief."

Cecilia shot up horrified. "Not the one that I've—" She dropped the handkerchief instantly on the ground, running from it. "Oh God."

"I held it to her mouth until she passed out and then I pushed her off the hill, and ran back through the hole in time for you and Miss Abbott to see me running down the stairs."

"Knowing we would assume that you couldn't have done because you'd have to walk past us in order to get to the Burton residence."

"That's right."

The doctor piped up, "But what about Jackie?"

"Well, that lends us to the second half of our story."

# Chapter 18
# Little White Pills

Miss Quinn never understood the concept of 'letting sleeping dogs lie', but as she stood surrounded by people who her revelations had ultimately hurt more than benefited, she knew she began to. And the longer she stood, the more she questioned her decision of coming back to this house. After all, she could've easily said her goodbyes, taken her train and kept her suspicions to herself.

She wondered what Rebecca would've wanted, or Jackie? She decided for her own peace of mind that they deserve the justice; then she took three deep breaths and continued.

"Now, back to Jackie's perspective. She shows up that morning ready to tell Rebecca the truth and let the pieces fall where they may. Only, she finds nobody standing on the cliff and leaning over, she spots Rebecca's dead body and screams. Her first thought being what a terrible, terrible thing she's done, driving a woman to suicide.

"A woman who was kind to her, gave her a home; she blames herself. Meanwhile, her scream alerts all of us and we all sprint to the scene of panic, as Eddie is with myself and Miss Abbott and has been for about twenty minutes, it strengthens his alibi. A couple of people lie about their whereabouts." She pauses briefly to skirt her eyes between Cecilia and Daniel.

"But that's neither here nor there. Anyway, detective arrives, etc. etc.; cut to the funeral. Now, we already know that the doctor was prescribing Jackie some sleeping pills for some no longer mysterious reasons, that we can assume she took religiously every night. Now at this point, I believe Eddie assumes he's gotten away with it; everyone lazily following with the story that Rebecca just jumped out of nowhere.

"That is until Jackie becomes so distraught believing that her blackmail is responsible for Rebecca's guilt and subsequent death. So distraught, she runs away from the funeral, quickly followed by me and Miss Abbott, and she confesses her sins ready to take her punishment. She finally reveals the truth as to why she came there in the first place, and we talk.

"I remember becoming so aware of how dark it was out there and I would be willing to bet anything that it was Eddie standing in the shadows. Now pinning Old Daniel's death on Rebecca would be one thing, but Jackie was remembering more, wasn't she? The funeral, the house, hell maybe even the pills brought back memories she didn't know she had and how long would it be until she figured out that Rebecca wasn't the one who killed her father, that it was you!"

Eddie once again frowned his head. "I panicked! I didn't know who she was going to tell, but I knew it wasn't going to be long before she figured it out."

"And everything you had worked so hard to build would come crumbling down. All because of some stupid mistake you made as a kid. So, what happened? What did you do?"

"I knew she was taking sleeping pills so ran up to her room, I took a few, definitely enough to make her faint but conscious. I crushed them up into her champagne."

"Jesus, she threw that drink back." The doctor leaned before finally sitting on the chair. "Oh God."

Eddie continued, "Everyone would either assume she was upset or drunk—"

"The glass, you collected everyone's glass but left hers on purpose so you would have a reason to go up there, didn't you?" Miss Quinn pressed.

Cecilia piped up, "And you needed a witness, didn't you? That's why I had to go up there with you! You traumatised me, for an alibi!" She stood agitated, held back only by Daniel's arms.

Miss Quinn turned. "Cecilia, think back; what happened when you went up there?"

"I don't know. God I was tired and I had some of that champagne and—"

Miss Quinn pressed, "Try, just try."

"We went up the stairs, Eddie being ahead of me. When we got up there, he was blocking my sight, I didn't see her until he moved slightly. Her head thrown back, that ghoulish purple overtone on her skin. God, I don't want to remember it!"

"And the pills? Do you remember the pills on the floor?" Miss Quinn questioned.

"Well, I knew they were there."

"No, forget that, did you see them?"

"I…I don't remember." She calmed, rubbing her head, sitting back down by the window.

Miss Quinn continued, "That's because they weren't really there at first, were they, Eddie?"

He lifted his head. "When Cecilia ran downstairs, I had less than a minute to pull out the sleeping pills and spill them everywhere before you all ran up."

"The light beige carpet creating the illusion they were always there, making us assume she overdosed. That quantity of sleeping pills couldn't possibly be taken accidently and that she knew what she was doing."

"Poor Jackie," the words came from Hugo, who had barely said a word all night. Miss Quinn tinged as she remembered the events she set into motion. Was this really better than living in a lie?

She continued nonetheless, "And then earlier this evening when it seemed to click in my head, we knew there was no proof of what Eddie had done, unless we caught him doing it again."

Daniel stood, owning his part of the story. "So, they came to me, told me everything. We figured if I could make a scene big enough to convince Eddie that I knew who the murderer was or that I would at least never stop searching, he would come after me too."

"Which he did, thankfully," Detective Carter who up until that had been a quiet observer, finally spoke up. He slowly stood with the officers he had standing side by side, until they peered closer and arrested Eddie. He was searched, read his rights and slowly taken out of the house, walking by everyone who once thought they knew him.

It was when he walked by Cecilia that he stood out of line, slapping him before the officers could even stop. She turned back to the door frame she was leaning on and wept, slowly being comforted by Eddie. Miss Abbott and Miss Quinn stood side by side and they watched Eddie disappear through the front door.

"What now?" Miss Abbott questioned.

"I'm not so sure." She looked at the scene around them. "Everyone seems so broken."

"You did the right thing."

"But Cecilia—"

Miss Abbott turned harshly. "You stopped that girl from marrying a murderer and don't you dare be sorry for that."

Miss Quinn rolled her eyes. "A rich murderer, at least give him some credit. What on earth will she do now?"

Miss Abbott peered at Cecilia whose tears were beginning to dry. "I don't know, I think she's much more resilient than we give her credit for."

"Daniel?"

"He has closure. He knows what happened at least, and the same goes for Hugo."

"What about the doctor?"

"Well, we can only hope that his licence gets immediately revoked." Miss Abbott shrugged.

A slight inappropriate smile fell on Miss Abbott's lips. "You didn't get much of holiday after all, did you, Miss?"

"It's my own fault; have to stop poking around in other people's business first. They'll all be alright, won't they?"

Just as that question was asked, Hugo came up to them with a kind smile on his lips, and he shook their hands. "Thank you. That couldn't have been easy, but thank you."

"What happens now?" Miss Quinn inquired.

"Well, you two are welcome to stay with us for as long as you need."

"That's kind, but I think we've overstayed our welcome just enough."

"Well, beyond that, we'll have to think of what to do with Rebecca's house. I doubt Daniel would want it after everything. It would be nice to find some way to honour her memory. Cecilia is also welcomed to stay as long as she likes, but I doubt she has many happy memories left here. I can tell you one thing though, the first that's coming down is that awful, wretched wall."

"I think Rebecca would approve of that."

He smiled before leaning away to talk to the doctor.

Daniel was the next to approach them. "I suppose I wanted to thank you as well."

"I suppose I should accept that," Miss Quinn retorted.

Miss Abbott piped up. "So, what are you going to do now?"

Daniel paused before looking around. "I don't know. It occurred to me that I haven't cared about what happens to me for a very long time. But I think giving up drinking and gambling is a good start, finally make my mother proud."

"And you and Cecilia?" Miss Quinn's eyes wavered over to her.

"No, I mean I still love her, but I know we're not right for each right now. But I'm going to work on that, becoming a better person every day, and who knows maybe one day, we'll bump into each other." He narrowed his eyes carefully. "I believe that if people are meant for each other, they'll find their way back eventually."

"That's beautiful, Daniel." Miss Abbott smiled.

"Yeah well, only sobriety for me from now on."

It was around ten minutes later when Miss Quinn and Miss Abbott ventured downstairs once again, with their bags packed and coats on, they said their goodbyes, and thanks and best wishes. They boarded the boat once again and spent the journey turning to look at the little rock they were swimming away from, until the boat captain finally piped up.

"Hey, I remember you! How was your holiday?"

Neither knowing exactly how to answer, Miss Quinn only replied, "Oh, I think you'll hear about it tomorrow."

# Chapter 19
# The Morning Paper

**20 July 1936**

*Burton Estate to be Turned into Orphanage!*

*After the tragic events concerning both the Burton and Newham Estates two years ago, the town proudly announces the opening of a new home for children. This Sunday past, Daniel Burton stood at the forefront of history in this town as he announced the opening of 'Rebecca Burton's Home for Children'; named after his mother who tragically died this summer two years ago.*

*The young Mr Burton now honours her memory by opening his estate up to the town. In addition to his own, he used his inheritance to purchase the Newham estate right next door and started construction right away! This reporter finds that the first thing to be demolished was the wall separating the two estates in order to create a big outdoor space for the children.*

*Now housing and schooling the town's youth, Mr Burton claims to only employ the best teachers from the mainland and to facilitate a safe, engaging learning space for the children. His father, Hugo Burton, recovering from a recent heart attack has been encouraged to rest, but will be joining the* faculty in the autumn as the head of engineering. For now, reports have shown that he works on building safer, engaging educational toys for the younger children housed in the orphanage.

This reporter is also happy to note that the elder Mr Burton seems to be recovering well and has thankfully changed his medical clinic. As following reports of gross incompetence last summer Dr White has had to liquidate his practice on account of having his medical licence revoked. Thankfully, he still lives peacefully on the edge of town. Sources say he has taken quite well to his new retired life and seems to best almost anyone at bingo!

Speaking of the events of last year, this reporter would like to remind anyone still wondering of the outcome of the trial of Edward Newham, caught literally red handed, the poor man didn't stand a chance in court and was sentenced to three life sentences. After being forced to spend the money he had left on lawyers, he had no choice but to sell the deed to his estate over to young Mr Burton, who if truth be told, was rightfully ruthless in court.

As to his very young and very beautiful fiancée, Miss Cecilia Winters began training as nurse in St Anne's Hospice not long after the events. Her quote that she wanted to 'prevent any more deaths' stuck with anyone present in the courtroom.

As to her exposed love affair with the younger Mr Burton (if we can be clear on what transpired, which we are certainly not), sources close to both Nurse Cecilia and Mr Daniel Burton say they still remain friends, with Mr Burton being a generous benefactor to St Anne's Hospice, but who knows, *perhaps Nurse Cecelia may inevitably join Rebecca Burton's Home for Children as an inhouse nurse for the children.*

Miss Quinn put down the paper and grasped the morning coffee in her hand—it was presently just past two in the afternoon—but Miss Quinn remarked it was always good to be optimistic. Miss Abbott lay waiting for her response, with eager eyes across the dining room table.

"Well, I think it's absolutely marvellous! Some good finally coming from that place."

"Oh no, not that!" Miss Abbott huffed in frustration.

"Was that not your question?"

"You know perfectly well it was not!" Miss Abbott leaned closer. "So, do you think they'll get together?"

"Lottie, I know you want to believe that love solves everything, but well, we don't even know *if* they love each other anymore."

"Maybe you're right, but I refuse to believe that feelings like that just go away." Lottie huffed again before placing her hands back on the paper and reading the article once again.

She barely noticed when Miss Quinn stared out of the window next to her. She hated to admit it but she was curious. She wondered if Lottie was right. If one day, Daniel and Cecilia would come back to each other as entirely different people. She wondered that if the mind is fully capable of repressing things that overwhelm it, that challenge and depress it; then why can't the heart do the same.

What is the reality of a possibility of a tiny space in your heart filled with locked boxes of pieces of your broken heart? While the people around you walk holding the keys. She wondered if one day, perhaps in the quiet corridor of Rebecca

Burton's Home for Children, they might pass each other, and recognise each other as the people they once loved. They had never said goodbye to each other, not really.

She wondered if they ever would. Perhaps they didn't remember what it was like to live before their game; she envied them and pitied them all at once. Someone worth being attached to, sacrificing yourself for—they had found that, and like most people, they were going to die in it if they had to. It had killed Eddie; she saw it in his eyes that very last day. It decayed him from the inside out, and then it killed Rebecca.

She wondered how much danger Cecilia and Daniel were in now. She shrugged her shoulders; none that she could save them from she supposed. It was a funny thought to her at that moment, that all humans walk around slightly in the line of danger; always slightly entangled, and always slightly at risk with anchors pulling them to one another.

We attach these hooks on ourselves and have the audacity to be surprised when we're reeled in. We struggle perhaps, maybe we skin and scruff ourselves trying to stay afloat, but the scariest notion is of those who willingly fall under, with a smile on their faces. She wondered if they were all still smiling when they resurfaced? Is it in human nature to have gratitude for the fleeting feelings that nearly destroy us; that remind us that we're still alive?

She wondered who her hooks were attached to, and who they would eventually pull in; refusing even in the safety of her mind to entertain the vulnerability that some people may have their hooks on her.